My Secret Dragon

Debbie Thomas

Little
Island

MY SECRET DRAGON

First published in 2018 by
Little Island Books
7 Kenilworth Park
Dublin 6W
Ireland

ISBN: 978-1-912417-06-3

A British Library Cataloguing in Publication record for this book is available from the British Library.

Cover illustration by Tom Bonson
Insides designed and typeset by www.redrattledesign.com

Printed in Poland by Drukarnia Skleniarz

Little Island receives financial assistance from
The Arts Council/An Chomhairle Ealaíon and the Arts Council of Northern Ireland

10 9 8 7 6 5 4 3 2 1

For Mum and Dad

YOU WIN,
CHARLOTTE FLYNN

Flying is overrated. I don't mean sitting in an aeroplane while it roars above the clouds. I don't mean hang-gliding or hot-air ballooning. I mean the bird kind, on feathery wings that soar and swoop and beat against the wind. When it comes to superpowers, flying's way down the list. And believe me I know about superpowers.

No-one *will* believe you, Aidan show-off Mooney, unless you stop boasting and start at the beginning.

Excuse me, Charlotte know-all Flynn, you're interrupting my story.

Our story, you mean.

Says who?

Says me. And without me, you'd be lying at the bottom of the Atlantic Ocean saying nothing at all, so says you too.

Fair point I suppose . . . for a girl.

How about you tell your parts, I tell mine?

Your small parts.

Small but crucial. Go on, say it.

Sigh. Small but crucial.

And what about the diary I rescued after the fire? Isn't that crucial too?

OK, you win. *Our* story.

SERIOUSLY?

It was the last day of the summer holidays and I was mad. Not because it meant the end of freedom and the start of homework but because it didn't.

'Why can't I go to school?' I was sitting at the kitchen table making sandwiches with Mum. Well, she was making them while I rammed them into a lunchbox, spilling half their hammy guts.

'Aidan.' She dotted lumps of hard butter on a slice of bread. 'You know why.'

Of course I did. 'But it's so unfair.'

'It's not about fairness,' she said quietly. 'It's about safety.'

'Not mine.'

Her knife slipped and tore a hole in the bread. 'Please, love. Let's go and have a nice picnic.'

How could I, when I knew she was just trying to distract me? Tomorrow, all over Ireland, other twelve-year-olds would be walking into classrooms, opening maths books, supergluing teachers to toilet seats or whatever they did in school. How would I know? I'd never set foot in one.

'I mean, what's your plan?' I squashed the living daylights out of another sandwich. 'If you don't think primary school's safe, you'll never be OK with secondary. So you'll keep me at home till I'm eighteen? You can't stop me leaving then. And how will I be ready if I've hidden away all my life –' my brain said *Stop right there*, but my tongue was on a roll, 'because of *your* problem?'

Mum's face was turning red. Sweat crept on to her forehead. 'I'm sorry.' She let out a trembly breath. The butter melted into the bread.

I should have said, 'I'm sorry too. I know it's not your fault.' But it wasn't mine either. And it was ruining my life.

A tear slipped from her eye, trickled down and steamed off her cheek. She rushed to the sink. Filling a glass with water, she drank it in one gulp. There was a hissing sound. She leaned back against the sink and took deep breaths. I stared at my lap, unable to look at her. Silence roared round the kitchen.

Then she mumbled something so crazy I couldn't help looking up. 'What?'

'I said you're right.'

'About what?'

'School. You should go.'

I blinked. 'As in go? As in to school?' OK, not my

brain's finest moment. But after a year of begging, it needed time to take this in.

Mum nodded.

'You mean – seriously?'

'Mm-hmm.'

'This term?'

'Why not?'

'Mum, that's . . . you're . . . wow!' I ran around the table and hugged her so hard she squeaked. I was dying to ask why she'd suddenly changed her mind. But I couldn't risk her changing it back, so I settled for more hugging and squeaking.

Good move. Perhaps because I didn't ask, she told me. Or perhaps she was telling herself, just to be sure. 'I've tried to ignore it, but the truth is you're getting too advanced for homeschool. I've been worrying about it all summer. There's not much more I can teach you. And you've just put it so –' she pressed her lips together, as if to squash the word she'd been going to use, 'clearly. Yes, it is my problem. And no, it isn't fair to hold you back. There's nothing wrong with you, and you're old enough to keep my secret now.' She smiled, using funny little muscles that made her look brave and scared at the same time. 'Aren't you?'

'Course I am! You can trust me completely, Mum.' I hugged her again.

'I know. It's other people I can't trust.' She pulled away. 'I mean imagine if someone found out. They might lock me up, or turn me into a freak show, or –'

'They won't!' I cut in before she could talk herself out of it. 'I'll guard your secret with my life.' I made fists with my hands and punched at the fridge. I shot the oven with finger-guns and blew pretend smoke from the barrels. I drew an air sword and stabbed the toaster. When I'd killed most of the kitchen, Mum smiled again. And this time all the muscles were brave.

It took a week of Googling, phoning and driving around to find a school we liked the look of. It took another week for St Malachy's Primary to decide that, yes, they had room for one more in sixth class. Then there were books and uniform to buy. So it was nearly three weeks before I woke up to the most exciting day of my life.

And your mum said there was nothing wrong with you? I mean what the Hades is exciting about school? The pushing in the corridor? The not-quite-whispers behind your back? The jokes about your lunch, your glasses, your fat legs? The lessons are pretty useless too. Hercules didn't need to spell 'Hesperides' to steal the golden apples. Achilles didn't beat the Trojan army with his neat handwriting.

Talking of handwriting . . . the diary I found starts around then.

September 18th

And so it begins. After five years of planning and a lifetime of learning, it's a dream to be here at last. Stepping off the plane this morning, I felt the layers of legend beneath my feet and smelt hope in the cold, sharp air. It's a hope that fuels my courage. Operation Zoe will demand all my mental and physical talents — maybe my life too. If I die, all I ask is that whoever finds this diary will use it to tell the world of my sacrifice. Books, films, statues — maybe an airport or two — will immortalise my mission to save the human race.

I'LL BE GRAND

Mum's glove felt warm and smooth. At least, that's what I imagined. You can't *actually* hold your mother's hand on the way to school. Even I knew that, which was pretty impressive for my first day. But it was good to have it there, along with the rest of her, as we turned the corner and St Malachy's came into sight.

Until I looked along the pavement. Only the smaller kids were attached to parents. The ones my size were strolling together towards the school gates, all chatter and laughter.

'Bye, Mum,' I said.

'What?' Now she grabbed *my* hand. And for the record her glove *was* warm and smooth. 'Don't you want me to come in? Help find your classroom, meet your teacher?'

'No, no and um . . .' I pulled my hand away, 'no. But thanks for the offer.' Mum's a great believer in thanksing. 'I'll be grand.'

'Course you will.' Mum leaned forward to kiss me. I stepped back. She patted my shoulder instead and gave a quick smile. 'I'll be here at three. Have a great day.' She sniffed and pressed her gloved fingertips to her cheekbones.

As she turned to go, a car drew up along the kerb. The back door flew open, hitting her arm. A boy got out. He blew up his mega-long fringe and headed through the school gates.

The driver leaned across. 'Sorry,' he said to Mum. 'My son can't see a thing through that mess.' He frowned. 'I don't think we've, ah . . .'

'We're new,' she mumbled. 'I mean Aidan is. Today. Nice to meet you.' She slammed the car door and hurried off down the pavement.

Oh no. I ran through the gates, praying that no one had seen the steam rising from her cheeks.

I saw you from across the road. Not the gloves or the steam but all that lovey stuff, before the car pulled up and blocked my view. I remember thinking how pukey, and how my dad hadn't walked me to school since third class.

WHY THE BIG SECRET?

When I was small, I didn't think Mum had a problem. I thought she was normal. I thought all mothers had blue-green scales on their hands, and feet that ended in curved white claws. I must have been three or four when I began to wonder why other women only wore gloves in winter and had hands the colour of old fudge.

At first I didn't mind that Mum was different. In fact I liked it. When she shed a scale I'd hold it up to the light, admiring the oily gleam, before storing it in my piggy bank. I wanted to tell all the people I met – which wasn't many – that she could breathe the perfect size flame to melt a single marshmallow, or snort out the right amount of smoke to cook six sausages. I didn't understand why she always wore gloves outdoors, and indoors too when the plumber or the electrician came. I didn't know why I was forbidden to tell a soul that she could light the sitting-room fire with her breath. But I knew it would upset her if I did, and that was enough to keep me quiet.

When I was six she tried to explain. But I still didn't get it. Perhaps I hadn't met enough people to know what they can be like.

'Some might find it . . . strange,' she said.

'Good strange or bad strange?' I mean, what could be cooler – or hotter, I guess – than being part-dragon?

She sighed. 'People often have trouble with things they can't understand.'

'Why?' Imagine a world without mystery. What a lump of soggy chips.

But I got the point. From then on, mum was the word on all things dragonoid. Which made her the problem too. If I met other children in the playground, she never chatted to their mums or invited them home. When I played football on the green, she wouldn't let the neighbouring kids come in, so they stopped inviting me round. The film of my life so far? *Homeschool Alone* starring Aidan Mooney. Featuring Mum, Nando and Gramps. Special Guest Disappearance by Dad.

Now I'd made it to school at last, and still Mum was causing trouble. I hadn't even got through the gates without an incident of public evaporation.

I took a deep breath and followed the crowd into the entrance hall. The long-fringed boy came up. Oh no. What had he seen?

But instead of asking how Mum's face could be part of the water cycle, he said, 'Are you new?'

'Yes.' I nodded as if my head was on a spring.

'Which class?'

'Miss Burkitt.'

'The Berk?' He grunted. 'Me too.' He headed off down the corridor.

I hurried after him. 'My name's Aidan.'

'Phil,' he said over his shoulder. That didn't surprise me. Cool boys always have names you can shorten to one syllable: Rob or Dave or Mike. And it turned out that Phil was as cool as Christmas. Walking into the classroom, he seemed to suck boys towards him like a Hoover gathering dust.

'Hey, Phil.'

'Howaya, Phil?'

I stood behind him grinning madly.

'Who's that?' someone said.

Phil glanced at me. 'Aidan. He's new.'

The three boys crowding round him didn't introduce themselves. But as I stood there with my lips stretched round my teeth, I caught their names from the conversation: Dan, Ben and Tom. A classful of cool. I cursed my extra syllable.

At last Phil turned to me. 'Why are you starting now? It's the third week of term. Did you oversleep?' His friends laughed. 'Or did they chuck you out of your last school?'

I swallowed. 'No. I was homeschooled.'

Phil widened his eyes at Tom, or was it Dan? 'Why?' he said. 'Problems?' He tapped his temple with a fingertip.

The others laughed again.

"Scuse me,' squeaked a voice from behind. I moved aside to make way for its owner.

'Breathe in, lads,' Phil said, 'it's the Chublotte.' The girl scowled and pushed past. She had thick glasses and mad coils of rust-coloured hair. The other boys sniggered.

I felt myself blush, as if I was the one who'd insulted her. 'Sorry,' I mumbled. But she'd already marched off. I followed her to a desk by the window. As she sat down, I pointed to the desk beside her. 'Can I sit here?'

I was only trying to be nice. But the way she glared at me, you'd think I'd strangled her kitten. I went and sat at the desk behind.

Number one, I haven't got a kitten. Number two, you'd have glared too if you'd just been insulted. And number three, I always sat alone so that no one would see me sneak-reading *Greek Gods and Heroes* during maths.

HANDS UP

The teacher came in. At the front desk she turned and clapped her hands. 'Settle down, everyone.' She was small with short grey hair. I imagined her neat kitchen cupboards, full of spices in alphabetical order. Her quick, dark eyes scanned the room and stopped at me. 'Ah, there you are.' She smiled. 'A special welcome to our new boy, Aidan Mooney.'

She made everyone clap and me stand up. Then she gave a speech about helping me to settle in and feel at home. I blushed and smiled and didn't point out that I'd never been anywhere less like home.

The morning was crazy with newness. I'd expected some of it: new faces, new names, a new building to find my way round. But there were other new things I hadn't imagined. The collar and tie imprisoning my neck. Sitting at a desk all morning instead of getting up to ice a cake or feed the birds. And hands. How was I supposed to know they went up?

'We have some exciting news,' Miss Burkitt said. 'St Malachy's has signed up for Green Schools, the national scheme that shows we care about the environment. Our theme this term is biodiversity.'

There was a loud yawn.

Miss Burkitt raised her eyebrows. 'Would you like to tell us what biodiversity means, Philip Pardoe?'

'No thanks.' He grinned. There were sniggers.

'I will.' I stood up. Here was a chance to prove I wasn't dumb, that homeschooling had made me as smart as anyone. 'It's all the different kinds of life.' I walked to the front. 'My mum and I did this biodiversity test in the garden. We put a square frame on the grass and counted every species of plant and insect we found inside it. Then we –'

'Thank you, Aidan.' Miss Burkitt cleared her throat. More giggles went round. 'Very good. You can sit down now. And please remember to put up your hand next time. We don't just walk around in class.'

'Oh.' I looked round at the grinning faces. Phil was sniggering and nudging Tom. 'Sorry.'

More laughter slid into my ears. My throat filled with carpet. I crept back to my desk.

'So,' Miss Burkitt said, 'biodiversity is very important. We need all the different plants and animals to keep the planet in balance. And sad to say, humans have done a lot to mess that balance up. How?'

I had some ideas but no way was I opening my mouth again.

'Yes, Charlotte?'

'Global warming,' came the squeaky voice in front of me. 'Using up fossil fuels. Hunting animals to extinction.'

'Excellent,' Miss Burkitt said.

Across the room, I saw Phil whisper something in Tom's ear. Tom smirked.

'For homework,' Miss Burkitt went on, 'I want you to look at extinction. Choose a species that's been wiped out by humans and write some notes on it to present to the class tomorrow.'

When the bell rang for break, everyone poured into the yard. Kids surrounded me, asking where I lived, what my favourite pizza was, what team I supported. They introduced themselves and offered to show me round.

At least they should have. That's what I'd imagined for the last three years. Not me standing by the fence, watching other boys play football.

I took a deep breath. 'Can I play?' I asked no one in particular.

Phil stopped the ball with his foot. 'Shouldn't you be counting earthworms?' The others laughed.

'Nerd,' he added.

Another boy from my class was standing on the sidelines: Conor something, with sticky-out teeth. He glanced at me. I smiled back like I'd won the Lotto, though it felt like my face was ripping.

Someone else looked my way, too. That girl with eyes like angry Maltesers. She was sitting by the fence, reading.

Well guess what I saw when I looked up from *Greek Gods and Heroes*? Blinky-blue eyes in a scared, sad face. I went back to Theseus slaying the minotaur. Now *there* was a guy who could handle a bully.

September 21st

At last she's arrived – my Hestia, my beauty, my hope for a future that will never end. It's hard to believe that she's living and breathing in front of me, delivered this morning by my Egyptian handler. But believe I must, for the sake of Operation Zoe and the whole of humankind. And as she pecks and flaps in her cage, her wings blaze as brightly as the brilliance of my plan.

HOMEWORK

After the morning disaster, I needed a plan for lunch break. The cool gang had made it clear I wasn't worth knowing. Fine. I'd try the uncool ones, the others left out of Phil's game that was in full swing again.

The other boys, you mean.

OK, I saw you by the shed, still reading. Or rather I saw your hair. You didn't look up. And I was hardly going to invite a bunch of arguing bedsprings, especially after their owner had laser-glared me off at small break.

'Want a kickaround?' I asked Conor, whose surname I now remembered was Murphy.

He pointed to his chest. 'Me?'

We found Kennedy Adoti kicking a ball against a wall. David Something and Andy Somethingelse were messing by the fence. We played all break. They weren't that good, but at least they smiled and it filled up the time.

At the end of school I went through the gates, past parents and waiting cars. I turned down a side road where I'd arranged to meet Mum, partly because of her shyness and partly because I knew she'd have to hug me.

Walking home, she shot out questions faster than I could answer them. 'What's your classroom like?'

'It's got desks facing the front and –'

'What are they like?'

'Just tables with –'

'Where do you hang your coat . . . eat your lunch . . . go to the bathroom?'

You'd think she'd have asked about my classmates, the teacher, the work. But Mum had more basic things to catch up on when it came to school.

We were at the front door by the time she got round to people. 'Make any friends?'

'Mmhh.' My voice sounded like a toilet recovering from a flush. No way could I tell her about Phil and his gang; she'd call it bullying and have me back homeschooling like a shot.

'And the lessons?' She dug in her bag for the key.

'Grand.'

She unlocked the door. 'Got any homework?'

'Yep.' Then it hit me. A chance to make up for my terrible start, to impress the class with something

I knew more about than all of them put together. I told her my idea.

Her back went stiff. The key froze in the lock. 'No,' she whispered. She pushed the door open and pulled me inside. 'You can't be serious.' She slammed the door, clapped a gloved hand to her mouth and ran to the kitchen.

'Mum.' I stood in the doorway as she rushed to the sink. She poured a glass of water and drank it in one gulp to quench the flame that had sprung from the edge of her mouth. 'I wouldn't talk about you. Course not.'

She pointed to the biscuit tin on top of the fridge. She sat at the table and took quick, hissy breaths while I brought down the First Day flapjacks we'd made to celebrate this moment. But the Ribena-raisin combo tasted soggy and sad and anything but a celebration.

'I'd write about dragons in general,' I said, 'not you in particular.' I dented a flapjack with my thumb. 'Obviously.'

'Oh, Aidan.' Mum pulled off her gloves. She sliced her flapjack into quarters with a claw. 'Think it through.' She speared a piece with her claw tip and slid it off with her teeth, like a sausage from a cocktail stick. 'At best your teacher will think you've confused extinct with imaginary. And at worst . . .' She frowned. 'She might ask why you believe dragons once existed. What if you let something slip?'

'Never! I'm not stupid, Mum. This is just a chance to clear things up. I'd explain that dragons weren't all horrible like the stories say.' I didn't add that it was also a chance to prove myself with the class. 'Some of them must have been like you – good at history and cheesecakes.'

It was meant to make her smile but instead her frown deepened. 'You see. That's just the kind of thing you might say by accident.'

As if. But the look on her face made me drop it. I'd got what I'd wanted for years – her permission to start school – and I shouldn't push my luck. Though after the day I'd had I wondered what kind of luck it was.

I went upstairs and Googled 'extinct animals'. I ended up choosing the yawny old dodo.

Well, I picked the Steller's sea cow, a whaley creature from a group of mammals called Sirenians after the Ancient Greek Sirens. Goodness knows why; the Sirens were beautiful maidens who sang to sailors and caused shipwrecks, while the sea cows were ten-ton lumps that moved so slowly they were hunted to extinction in twenty-seven years.

NOT SO HAPPY BIRTHDAY

If Nando and Gramps had got their way, I wouldn't be here at all.

Don't get me wrong. My grandparents adore me. I'm not just their only grandchild, I'm also a huge relief. When I was born with everything in order, they must have felt like . . . well, like they'd found a bathroom after nine months of bursting. They'd been dead against Mum having a baby, which is why they'd been dead against her marrying Dad. Again don't get me wrong. They liked him a lot, at least at first. What they didn't like – what in fact they hated – was the thought of Mum passing on her genes.

So did Dad, as it turned out. He must have loved Mum to start with because, when he found out about her 'thinginess' (as he apparently called it), he promised (so she says) to protect her for ever from the big, wide, shockable world. And when she got pregnant, he jumped (so she tells me) for joy and said he'd love me just the same if I had thingy parts or not.

Yeah right. What's that saying again? If you can't stand the heat, get out of the kitchen. Well Dad couldn't, literally, so he did, also literally, one morning when Mum was six months pregnant. And he didn't stop there but carried on down the hall, opened the front door, went along the pavement, turned left at the Spar, met Someone Else, got divorced and emigrated to New Zealand. The way Mum tells it, you'd think everything happened in one day. So all I know of my father is Mum's sad memory and, according to her, enough maintenance money to 'keep our heads above water'.

Thanks for nothing, Dad – except your ordinary genes.

Back to those extraordinary ones. As I said, Nando and Gramps didn't want Mum to pass them on. Pretty rich, I know, when they'd given them to her in the first place. But they didn't know that until she was born. Like me, they don't have a trace of thinginess, at least not on the outside. I started wondering about that a couple of years ago. Why was she the only one?

I Googled stuff on genes and learned that they can hide in families for generations and then reappear, apparently out of the blue. There have been dark-skinned babies born to light-skinned parents, and the other way round, because two people of different skin colour got together generations ago. And – take a deep breath – some babies are born with tails. Now take a deeper one – that's because we all had one once. Me, the postman, Cristiano Ronaldo: every human embryo has a tiny tail that's absorbed by the body as it grows. Even after birth, our tail bone sits at the bottom of our spine, like a Post-it note reminding us of our animal ancestors.

In Mum's case, though, it wasn't just tails or skin colour. It was more than different race or even species. When she was born, it seemed to my grandparents that fact and fiction collided.

At first, Nando and Gramps thought their baby was deformed. That's not my word. But I can't blame Nando for thinking it when she saw the scales that covered Mum's hands and feet like polished bruises, and the moon-white claws in place of fingers and toes. I can understand why she needed to have a little scream while the no-nonsense midwife did the usual checks for breathing and reflexes. Then Nurse Shauna McHale wrapped Mum up, popped her into Nando's arms and waddled out to tell Gramps that his brand-new daughter was exceptionally beautiful.

'Meringue,' Nando told me. 'That's the colour he went when he saw your mum's hands and feet.'

Nurse Shauna agreed not to tell the doctors until Nando and Gramps had adjusted to the particular beauty of their child. 'She's passed all the tests,' she said. 'So there's nothing wrong. You tell me when you're ready to show her to a doctor.'

Not in an hour. Not in four. When it was time to go home, 'ready' still hadn't tapped them on the shoulder.

'Grand,' said Nurse Shauna. 'I'll come and visit you, make sure the baby stays healthy. Beyond that, she's none of my business. Or anyone else's,' she said firmly, patting Nando's arm, 'if that's the way you want it.'

Nando cried and hugged her. And it was the nurse's turn to cry when Nando named the baby Shauna. Then Nurse McHale waddled away from the most fabulous delivery of her life.

Mini-Mum was gorgeous. The photos are all squashy smiles, not a scale or claw in sight. Nando and Gramps hid them under babygros and blankets. They considered taking her to a doctor. But Nando told me that Mum was so happy they couldn't bear the thought of worried frowns and millions of tests. I have another theory. It was really her 'deformity' that my grandparents couldn't bear. By hiding it they could escape their embarrassment and shame.

It was only when Mum turned two that they

had a spark, so to speak, of understanding. And that was only thanks to one of those amazing coincidences that tell reason to pack its bags and leave by the back door because wonder is knocking at the front.

Mum's back teeth had come through. She was chewing on a rattle and looking at a book with Nando. They happened to turn to a picture of a dragon just as Mum happened to chomp extra hard on her rattle. A spark flew from the side of her mouth.

After much shrieking (grown-up) and forced drinking of water (toddler), Nando phoned Gramps and ordered him home from the bank. 'Now, George. Right NOW.'

She sat him on the sofa with the dragon picture, and Mum on the floor with a rattle. After a minute, another spark shot from Mum's mouth. This one burst into a tiny flame at the edge of her lips. While Nando poured more water down her throat, Gramps picked up the rattle from the floor. He gasped at the dent where the plastic had melted.

It was five days before they could say the word 'dragon'.

Once they got over their shock – forget that, I don't think they ever did. But they did do their best. Nando became a health nut. She bought vitamins that failed to turn Mum's scales into skin, and tonics that couldn't stop her breathing fire. They knew it had something to do with her teeth. Dental check-ups were banned, of course, just like doctors' visits. They couldn't risk any 'experts' finding out and turning Mum into a freak show.

Instead, Gramps did his own research. To make fire, he figured, you need a spark and fuel. He looked into her mouth and noticed that her back teeth had grey flecks like tiny scattered fillings. He guessed they were bits of metal or flint that sparked when Mum ground them together. They prayed her adult teeth would be normal. But no, her permanent molars were completely grey. As for fuel, he worked out there must be gases in her mouth that burned when ignited. How they got there was anyone's guess.

Something tells me we're about to hear yours.

AIR BISCUITS AND POP TARTS

I'm not talking baking. I'm talking rump rippers, master blasts and butt yodels. Whatever you call them, Mum doesn't do them. I don't mean she goes into another room, or pretends it was the person next to her. I mean she never farts. Not now and, as far as we know, not ever. Nando and Gramps come from a generation that won't discuss it, but she's never so much as pip-squeaked or tooted in front of me.

OK, got the message. What's your point?

That most of us let our gas out from the basement but Mum stores hers in the sitting room.

You what?

I mean maybe there's some difference in her anatomy that keeps the gas inside, ready to rise into her mouth and catch fire. Only provable with X-rays and ultrasounds of course and, as I said, doctors were out of bounds. Whatever the process, all Nando and Gramps knew was that when Mum ground her teeth, fire came from her mouth. If they could stop the grinding, they thought, there'd be no spark.

Easier said than done. As well as grinding her teeth deliberately, Mum sometimes did it unintentionally, when she was excited or upset. Their solution was to raise her in a super-calm, super-quiet home. No loud music or sad stories, no play dates or parties. She was dressed in trousers and socks, long sleeves and gloves, before she stepped out of the door, never mind if it was a heat wave. Gramps bought every toy she wanted and arranged holidays on cool, remote islands. But the more she was protected, the less she felt accepted.

'Acceptance is different from love,' she told me. 'That I got in spades – hugs and kisses and kindness. But why did they move from Wales to Ireland, where they knew no one, when I was three? Why did Nando insist on homeschooling me? Why didn't they let me join Brownies? Because they were ashamed of me.'

I hate to say it, but I knew how they felt.

THE A-TEAM

On Tuesday morning, I felt Phil's eyes on me as I headed to my desk. I looked straight ahead and gave a kind of breathy whistle, partly to show that I hadn't noticed him, and partly to drown out the insult that was no doubt coming my way. I was unpacking my bag when, oh no, he came over.

'Hey,' he said.

'Hey.' I peered into my bag. Where was my maths copy? I made a big fuss of rummaging around.

'You know yesterday? I was only messing.'

Ah, there it was, right at the bottom. I fished the book out and put it on my desk.

'Coz you're new and stuff.'

I looked up. He flicked his fringe from his forehead. 'I just . . . d'you wanna join us for football today?'

'Um. OK. Yeah.' Dammit, I'd answered too quickly. He gave a quick nod and went back to his desk.

I sat down. What was that about? Was he making fun of me? Or was this his way of saying sorry? He didn't seem the apologising sort. But whatever the reason, I wasn't going to refuse.

At break, as I walked towards Phil's crowd, Conor and Kennedy came up. Conor was holding a ball. He grinned and drop-kicked it to me.

'I'm, ah, with them today. Sorry.' I kicked it back. I swear Conor's teeth drooped. 'It's just Phil invited me.' I bit my lip. Eejit. As if that would make them feel better.

'OK.' Conor nodded quickly. Kennedy turned and marched off, as if he'd just remembered an urgent appointment.

'Sorry,' I said again to their backs. But I'd promised the A-Team. What else could I do?

I focused on the game. When my goal won the match, and Phil shouted, 'Legend!' I didn't feel so bad about letting the others down. The A-Team needed me.

We played again at lunch break. And at the end of school, Phil walked with me across the yard. I recognised his dad from the first day, waiting at the gate. He waved. That was nice. Maybe he was behind the overnight change. Maybe he'd told Phil to be kind to the new boy. I waved back.

'See you tomorrow,' Phil said, heading through the gate. And then the best word I'd ever heard: 'Aid.'

Boys are so simple. Knock off a syllable and they think they're part of the gang. Even if you could squash my name (Charl? Ott?), it wouldn't have won me friends. Not that I cared. More chance to finish *Greek Gods and Heroes* during break.

September 23rd

If God existed, I'd swear he was smiling down on me. My agents are in place across Europe, and Hestia and I are settling into our Irish home. High and remote, it's the perfect spot for Operation Zoe.

But of course there's no God, no higher power, only powers we haven't discovered. And it's up to mankind — or a special kind of man — to harness them for the good of humanity. So here I stand, at the gateway to Europe, on the edge of a revolution in evolution. And if I find what I'm looking for, every nation in the world will soon be queuing up to support my work.

AT THE PARDOES

Phil got friendlier as the week went on, which meant that Dan, Ben and Tom did too. At break on Thursday they invited me to play.

'Any time,' Phil said. 'You don't have to ask.' At lunch Tom and Dan saved me a place on their table. And in PE, Phil chose me for his Rounders team. By Friday, school was turning into everything I'd hoped for. The lessons were fine and, after a rocky start, I was getting the hang of friends.

The only thing I hadn't worked out was jokes. At home there were two kinds: funny or not. St Malachy's had a third kind – jokes that were *in*. They didn't have to be funny but they did have to skewer someone else.

Hmm, I wonder who for instance?

Look, I didn't like it. But how could I stop the others from whispering, 'Steller's sea cow' when you walked past our lunch table?

Duh – by telling them not to?

They'd have ignored me. And anyway, I wasn't going to risk losing the invitation I'd just got from Phil. I took a deep breath. It's hard to sound too keen when you're Hulking out your chest. 'To your house, you mean . . . just me?'

He nodded. 'My dad said tomorrow, if you're free.'

So that was it. Daddy feeling sorry for the new boy again. My chest deflated. Still, I wasn't going to refuse my first ever proper, non-family invitation.

I tried not to talk about it in front of the others in case Dan or Tom or any other syllables felt left out. I did notice a few envious glances, but they only seemed to encourage Phil.

'My mum asked what you want for dinner,' he said loudly during art that afternoon.

'Anything's grand.' I figured the honest answer might not be wise: chicken drumsticks barbequed for fifty-two minutes over Mum-fired charcoal.

At three o'clock on Saturday Phil's dad opened the door. He smiled. 'Aidan.' He was wearing a jacket and tie. Maybe he worked on Saturdays.

He glanced down the road in a way that made me feel I should explain. 'My mum dropped me off.'

'Ah. I'd have invited her in.' He held out his hand

as if I was the head of an oil company. He looked so smart and sorted, the kind of person who never had dirty fingernails or an overdue library book. We shook hands. 'Come in,' he said.

The hall had a cream carpet, so smooth it looked freshly poured.

'Philip!' he called. 'Aidan's here.'

Phil came downstairs, followed, I guessed, by his mum. She had a TV presenter kind of face with everything in the right place and lots of make-up.

'My wife,' said Mr Pardoe, again like I was a grown-up.

She wiggled her hand in a wave. Odd, I thought, how some women grew their nails to look like claws, while Mum hid her claws because they didn't look like nails.

'Make yourself at home,' said Mrs Pardoe. That would be hard. Home was wellies in the hall and coats thrown over the banister. She glanced at my feet: the tiniest movement, but enough to make me bend down and take off my shoes. She turned to Phil. 'Aren't you going to offer him a drink?'

The kitchen was all black and white. Black counter tops, white cupboards, black and white floor tiles.

'Milk?' Phil said. I nodded. He opened the fridge. 'Mam, there's no milk!'

She stuck her head round the door. 'Go and get some, then. And a packet of biscuits.' She held out a twenty euro note. 'I want the change, Philip.'

At the corner shop Phil took two Galaxy bars, two tubes of Pringles, a big bottle of Pepsi and, oh yes, some milk.

'Didn't your mum say . . . ?' I trailed off.

'She won't know.'

'But the change?'

'What change?' He grinned. 'I've just remembered she owes me pocket money.'

And I've just remembered I'm a purple aardvark.

Back at the house we went up to Phil's room and played on his X-box, licking our fingers so that chocolate wouldn't mess up the controller. After *Call of Duty* and a busload of sugar, I didn't feel like dinner. But I could hardly say no when Mrs Pardoe called us down.

She brought in serving dishes while we sat at the dining room table. It was all so perfect: the silver serviette rings and the glass water jug that reflected light from what you could only call a chandelier. Even the steam from the potatoes rose in neat spirals.

'So,' Mr Pardoe said. 'Aidan.' He held the jug high and poured water into my glass. 'I hope Philip's helping you to settle in at St Malachy's.'

I swallowed a mouthful of potato. 'He's been great.'

Mr Pardoe nodded in approval. 'And why exactly are you starting now?'

I explained about homeschooling: that Mum thought I'd learn faster at home, but now I wanted to get used to school before starting secondary.

'And your father?'

I didn't say that Dad was too busy living in New Zealand, with his wife-upgrade, to give a hoot about my education. I said, 'It's just me and Mum.'

'Ah.' His eyebrows met in a sympathetic way. 'So.' He dabbed his lips with a serviette. 'If you've been homeschooling, what will she do, now you're at St Malachy's?'

I hadn't given that a thought. I said the first thing that came into my head. 'She likes cooking.'

'Really?' He spread the serviette over his lap. Then: what kind of cooking, where did she shop, did she check the sell-by date on food?

I stopped chewing. 'Sorry?' This was getting weird.

'It's his job,' Phil said, slicing a piece of chicken.

'Oh.' I tried to look as if that explained everything.

I must have failed because Mr Pardoe put down his knife and fork. 'I'm an ENVIRONMENTAL HEALTH OFFICER.' I could hear the capital letters. 'I protect the health of Drumadea. Restaurants, hospitals, cinemas and so on. I check they're free of pollutants, contaminants, poisons, impurities and toxins.'

'Wow.' I cleared my throat. 'Amazing.'

'It is,' he said, though what really amazed me was that he could think of five words that meant the same thing.

'Take a fridge.' He reached for his glass and took a sip of water. 'It's a breeding ground for germs. My job is to see they don't, ah, germinate.' He chuckled.

'A vital service,' said Mrs Pardoe.

He put the glass down. 'And risky. We're always hearing about this brave garda or that heroic fireman. But their enemies are obvious.' He took his knife and pointed it at me. 'Mine lurk invisibly in the microwaves and dishwashers of Drumadea.'

I pictured armies of bugs in tiny helmets and boots marching across café tables.

'And you know how germs spread?' He waggled the knife. 'By doubling. Two, then four, eight, sixteen, thirty-two . . . before you know it, there are millions of microbes infecting our buildings. And not just the public ones.' He shook his head. 'You wouldn't believe the muck some people live in.'

I blinked at my plate and pictured the dirty socks on my bedroom floor, the apple core on my desk, the cup that was stuck to my bedside table.

After dinner Mr Pardoe offered to take me home. I sat in the front of their BMW. It smelt of new shoes in a pine forest. He parked outside our gate and opened his door.

'I've got a key,' I said quickly. 'Mum's probably asleep. Thanks a mil.' I jumped out before he could ask why she'd be in bed at half past seven. I ran down the drive, hoping it was too dark to make out more than the shape of our twelve-year-old Skoda, and spent ages unlocking the door.

Mum was standing in the hall. 'How did it go?' She held out her arms. My first invitation had been a big deal for her too.

'Great.' I dodged her hug. Her dressing gown was wonky. She must have been washing up because her sleeves were wet. A claw tip poked through one of her slippers. Outside, the BMW purred off down the road. Why couldn't she do up her dressing gown properly? Why was she *in* her dressing gown? Why did she never wear make-up? I ran upstairs to my bedroom and slammed the door. Why was she born such a freak?

How could you use that word? How could you even think it?

October 4th

An excellent morning with the local cops. Sergeant Barry had no problem with the delay in my CIA clearance, especially after I offered him a personal gift for keeping things quiet until the paperwork comes through. Then it was all, 'Yes sir, no sir, wipe your nose sir.' He's done me and the world a favour by promising to cooperate in any way he can.

Most everything's in place now, except for my subjects, and I hope we'll find some soon. A nurse too; I'll need to hire someone local and discreet who can get hold of medical supplies without raising eyebrows.

A BIG ASK

Now it was my turn. I had to invite Phil back. That's how friendship worked. Or rather, normal friendship. When your mother's ten per cent fairy tale, normal goes up in smoke.

Ha ha.

It wasn't funny, believe me. I slipped in the question before school on Monday. I was putting on my coat while she fetched my lunchbox from the kitchen.

'What?' She came into the hall.

'Next Saturday,' I said, grabbing my schoolbag. 'Just for a few hours.'

She handed me my lunchbox. 'You know that's impossible, Aidan.'

'Why?' I shoved the box in my bag. 'It's what friends do, Mum. It'll be fine. Just wear your gloves.'

'But what if they slip? Or what if I . . . ?' She

circled her hands in in front of her mouth, which I guessed meant 'breathe fire'.

'Stay in your bedroom. Keep out of the way.'

Her shoulders gave a little twitch. 'But he might want to meet me. Or his parents might.' She held out my bag. 'What if there's an emergency? It's too risky, love.'

'What the hell?!' I hiked the bag on to my shoulder. 'Why bother letting me start school, then? You've got to have friends back, Mum, or they stop being friends. It's a two-way thing.' I pushed past her to the door. 'Not that you'd know. Or care.' I reached for the handle. 'I wish Mrs Pardoe was my mum!'

She stared at me.

'I –' My hand froze on the handle. 'I'm sorry. I didn't mean that.'

Of course I didn't. Mostly.

And of course she knew it – mostly. Her cheeks were going red. I dropped my bag, dived into the downstairs bathroom and poured a glass of water (all the sinks in our house had emergency glasses). She drank it in one gulp. I dug my fingernails into my palms and wished I could shovel the words back in.

When her breathing had slowed, she cleared her throat. 'Well . . .' she blinked round the hall, as if she might find the rest of her sentence on top of the bookshelf or beside the phone. 'We'll have to clean the house from top to bottom, get rid of any loose scales. And think up a good story about why I wear gloves indoors.'

How about the oldest glove story in history? In the *Odyssey* by Homer, written two-and-a-half thousand years ago, Odysseus's dad Laertes wears gloves to protect himself from brambles. On second thoughts, I guess there aren't too many brambles inside the modern home.

MOCKING AND BAKING

I was a wriggle of nerves on Saturday morning.
As Mum and I cleaned up, I wondered if we could
move house before lunch. I'd never had a problem
before. I'd lived here all my life and the house was
part of me, as familiar and comfortable as my
nose. But now, for the first time, I noticed things.
The chipped tiles in the downstairs bathroom. The
bran flakes I'd flicked on the kitchen ceiling two
years ago to test their sticking power. The coffee
stain on the sitting room carpet. Hoovering and
dusting felt like putting a plaster on an ankle after
the foot's fallen off.

Mum so didn't help. 'Have you planned what to
do?'

'I've got some ideas.'

'Are you sure he likes lasagne?'

'That's what he asked for.'

'What time is he coming?'

'I've told you three times,' I snapped. 'Four
o'clock.'

On the dot. When I opened the door, Phil and his dad were standing there.

'How are you, Aidan?' Mr Pardoe smiled. 'Is your mother there? I was wondering when to collect Philip.'

'She's busy. We'll bring him home about seven.'

When he'd gone, Mum came downstairs. We'd agreed she'd say hello then leave us to it. 'Hi, Phil,' she said. 'I'm Shauna.'

I followed Phil's gaze round the hall, noticing even more things I'd missed this morning, as if he'd lent me his eyes: the shelf I'd forgotten to dust, a cobweb the Hoover had ignored.

'What do you want to do?' I said. He shrugged.

'Go on the X-box?'

'What have you got?'

'Minecraft. Kinect.' He shook his head. 'Go outside? There's a basketball hoop. Or football on the green.'

'Nah.'

'How about a drink?' Mum said. She should be long gone. But I knew she was feeling my pain.

We sat at the kitchen table. Mum went to the fridge while I searched desperately for something to say.

Phil beat me to it. 'Why's your mum wearing gloves?' Just like that. As if she wasn't there. Wow.

'She . . . ah . . .' I'd expected the question but

not so soon. 'She's got eczema.' Mum opened the fridge. Thank goodness her back was turned.

'Eww,' he said. 'My auntie gets that. Looks gross.'

I laughed too loudly. 'Really gross. That's why she hides it.' I went to the fridge and took the lemonade bottle from Mum. 'See you later, then.'

She nodded and went to the door. 'Those biscuits you made are in the tin, Aidan. Help yourselves.'

Phil grinned. 'Hey, Aid, are you into baking?'

I didn't like his tone of voice. But Mum said, 'He loves it. He can do anything – brownies, muffins, bread. And he invents recipes.'

Get out of my life, my eyes begged her. But she was smiling at Phil.

'Coo-wul,' he said. 'Can he sew and knit too?'

'No,' I muttered. 'Let's go on the X-box.'

'Nah, let's bake.'

As Mum went out, he gave the secret smile of someone planning a serious slagging. 'How about some fairy cakes?'

I pictured him at school on Monday: *Hey Ben, guess what Aidan made me do at his house?*

'I don't know how,' I lied.

'Aww.' He sighed. 'You decide then. You're the expert.' He wasn't giving up.

A knot went tight in my chest. Fine. If that's what he wanted, he'd get my best. 'OK, we'll do a chocolate cream cake.' I went to the cupboard and brought out a packet of flour and a pot of hot chocolate powder.

'Where's the recipe?' he said as I put them on the table.

I fetched a mug and a mixing bowl. 'Put in two cups of flour and one cup of hot chocolate powder.'

While he measured them into the bowl I opened the fridge. There was no cream. No yoghurt either. Milk was too runny and the cream cheese had garlic in it.

'Mayonnaise?' Phil's spoon froze as I put a bottle on the table. 'In cake?'

I shrugged. 'Right colour. And it's got sugar in.' I was beginning to feel on safe ground.

Phil wrinkled his nose as if I'd just let rip. 'Sounds disgusting.'

I shrugged. 'If it is, we'll chuck it.' I squeezed the bottle.' I've invented lots of things this way.'

A blob farted into the bowl. Phil couldn't help laughing. 'More.'

I squeezed again. 'I made ketchup cake the other day.'

'What?'

'With cinnamon and nutmeg. Sweet and spicy.'

He looked unconvinced. But also slightly impressed. 'Doesn't your mum mind you messing?'

I laughed. 'She loves it. She gives marks out of ten. Eight to tens we put in the recipe book. If it's five to seven, we try again. One to fours we bin.' I fetched a jar of honey from the cupboard and put three spoonfuls in the bowl.

'Wow.' Phil went to the fridge. 'My turn.' He opened the door, looked inside and brought out the sweet chilli sauce. He blobbed some into the cake mix and stirred. The mockery had melted from his face.

Half an hour later I took a dark cake out of the oven.

'Let's get your mum,' he said. Before I could think of a reason not to, he was in the hall. 'Mrs Mooney,' he called.

She appeared on the landing. 'Everything OK?'

'We invented a cake,' said Phil. 'Will you mark it?'

I pulsed my eyes at her. 'It's OK, Mum. I know you're busy.'

'Please,' Phil said.

She laughed. 'OK, just for you.' She came downstairs. So much for keeping out of the way.

She cut a slice of cake and brought it to her mouth. She made a big show of holding it to her lips and making smacky sounds as she nibbled. She took another bite. A smile lit her face like a dimmer switch coming on. 'Wow. Nine point nine nine nine.'

Phil frowned. 'Why not ten?'

She sighed. 'Too small. I could eat two of them.'

'So let's make another one.' Phil grabbed the mayonnaise and squirted it into the bowl.

IN . . . AND OUT

'That was fun,' Phil said as we sat down to dinner. 'My mam would never let me mess like that. You guys have good ideas.'

Mum smiled as she put a plate of garlic bread on the table. 'Dig in,' she said.

Phil took a slice. 'Hey. Maybe you can help us with Halloween.'

'Sure,' Mum said. 'We always cook something special.' She went to the oven. The dish of lasagne sat steaming on top.

'I don't mean cooking.' Phil chewed his bread. 'I mean think up a trick for the Berk.'

'The Berk?' Mum's back was turned as she spooned lasagne on our plates.

'Miss Burkitt,' I said, taking a piece of bread.

'Something to get her back,' Phil said, 'for being such a dragon.'

I dropped my bread. There was a sound, *thuddump thuddump*, like a ball hitting a racket. My heart.

For an endless second it drowned out everything. Then Phil's voice came back. '... hard to scare her. She's pretty unshockable, don't you think?' He looked at me. 'What?'

I was staring at Mum's back. Go, I prayed. NOW. Her shoulders rose and fell with deep, careful breaths. In ... and out. In ... and out. I reached across the table and knocked over the water jug.

'Hey!' Phil jumped up.

'Sorry,' I lied, making a big deal of wiping it up with my serviette.

Mum turned round. 'Hmm,' she said softly. 'I wonder.' In ... and out. 'What could you do?' In ... and out.

I looked for the glow on her cheeks, the sweat on her forehead. Nothing.

She walked – not ran but walked – to the sink and poured a glass of water. Slowly she brought it to her lips. She drank half, then poured the rest away. 'Tricks,' she said. 'Not really my area. Can you think of anything, Aidan?'

'Um.' I swallowed. 'How about cobwebs round the classroom?'

Phil sat down again. 'Lame.'

Mum brought our plates over. 'Spider in the desk?' she said, putting them in front of us. A smile twitched the edges of her mouth.

I didn't know how, but the danger had passed.

'We did spiders last year,' Phil said. 'With Mrs

Hickey.' I pictured the fifth-class teacher, all nerves and perfume, fluttering along the corridor. 'Slow, children, slow.'

'It was brilliant.' Phil grinned. 'I got this remote-control tarantula off Amazon. And when she was writing on the board, I put it on the floor behind her. She turned round and it crawled on to her foot. She was like, "Aaagh!"' He jumped up again, clutching his face. 'She screamed so much the principal came in. Then she saw it was fake. She was so embarrassed. She yelled at us to tell her who'd done it. And guess who opened her big fat mouth? Charlotte swotface Flynn.'

'Oh.' I put down my fork. Now it made sense. 'That's why you hate her.'

He shrugged. 'Partly.'

For once I agree with Phil Pardoe. He hated me before that, too. Maybe he couldn't bear me coming top. Maybe he just didn't like my face. Whatever, he'd turned the whole class against me. I was an easy target: the weak floorboard he loved to step on. That's why I was glad to get him into trouble. Plus, I felt sorry for Mrs Hickey. She could have had a heart attack. Plus plus, what did I have to lose? Not friends, that's for sure.

FRIENDSHIP PIE

After dinner we invented dessert. Mum suggested Phil Pardoe pie, made from ingredients starting with P. I swear Phil actually blushed. Ten minutes later he was mixing popcorn with peanut butter, porridge oats and plain flour. I opened a tin of peaches.

The doorbell rang. Mum frowned at me. We weren't used to visitors.

'I'll get it.' I went down the hall and opened the door.

Mr Pardoe stood on the doorstep. 'I was called to inspect a restaurant this side of town so I thought I might as well collect Philip, save your mum a trip.'

'I'll go and get him,' I said, pushing the door towards him. 'Wait here a sec.' But he'd already stepped past me into the hall. What could I do but follow him down to the kitchen?

Phil switched off the hand mixer. 'Dad?'

Mum turned from the counter. 'Oh.' Her hand

flew to her head. 'How –' flour settled in her hair, 'how are you?'

Mr Pardoe glanced at her gloves.

'Eczema,' Phil said.

'Ah.' Mr Pardoe drew a breath. 'Sorry. Painful?'

'A bit.' Mum dropped her arms. 'Sometimes.' She put her hands behind her back. 'Not too bad.' She brought them to her sides again.

'Mum!' I smacked my forehead. 'You were meant to phone Gramps at six, remember?'

She blinked. 'Oh. Yes. Oh dear.' She wiped her gloves on her trousers. 'Sorry. You'll have to excuse me.'

'He's in hospital,' I lied as she went out.

Mr Pardoe looked round. He went to the counter, picked up a carton of milk and put it in the fridge. 'Shouldn't leave it out, you know.' He wagged a teacherly finger.

'Daaad.' Phil rolled his eyes. 'We're not done.'

'No problem.' Mr Pardoe folded his arms. 'I'll wait.'

'No,' I said quickly. 'Mum and I have to visit Gramps.' I'd had enough close shaves for one day. I needed them to go. 'I'll finish the pie and bring it in on Monday.' Now it was *my* turn to push past Mr Pardoe, and *he* had no choice but to follow.

In the hall he said, 'Could I just use your . . . ?'

I nodded and pointed to the downstairs bathroom.

While we waited, Phil put his coat on. 'That was loads of fun.'

'Really?' I felt a grin spill across my face. The mess, the mother, the moments of danger: suddenly they were all worth it.

When I'd closed the front door, Mum rushed downstairs. 'I did it!' she shouted, holding up her gloved hand. 'I stopped myself breathing fire!'

We high-fived. 'How?' I said.

She sat on the bottom stair. 'When Phil said "Dragon", I felt myself warming up. But for the first time ever, I knew how to stop it – maybe because I had to know. I took deep breaths and pictured the coldest scenes I could. Icebergs at the North Pole, snowfields in Alaska, the top of Mount Everest. Oh, Aidan.' Her eyes shone like green glass. 'I've spent my whole life hiding away, not daring to test myself in public. Now I have, and I passed!'

I hugged her. Because I'd passed too. An actual friend had come to my actual house and actually enjoyed it.

At least, he said he had.

I walked into class on Monday with a cake tin under my arm. I went up to his desk and opened the lid. 'Marks out of ten?'

He shook his head and turned to talk to Dan. At break, when I offered it again, he scrunched his nose and walked off.

'Phil?' I ran after him. 'What's wrong?'

'I don't want your pie, that's all.' He waved Tom over.

'You mean *yours*,' I said. 'Phil Pardoe pie, remember?' He put his arm round Tom and herded him away.

I ended up giving it to Kennedy Adoti. He offered me his crisps in return but I wasn't hungry. What on earth had I done wrong? Friendship was so confusing.

That's why I'd given up. I'd tried a few times. But I never knew where I stood with Ciara Kelly, and Louise Ryan said one thing to my face and others behind my back. What was the point? I was better off alone.

October 20th

Frustrated! More than a month in my new home and no real progress from my European agents. The only lead is from Derek, that small-town, small-minded creep. Should I take him seriously? He seems keener to disinfect the world than to work for its good. As my nearest agent, though, he'll be useful when the real work starts. And on the plus side, he's a sucker for following orders.

THE NEWS

On Monday evening it hit me why Phil had backed off. I was putting out the rubbish when the stink of the bin rushed up my nose. Of course. His dad. The messy kitchen, Mum's eczema, the milk left on the counter, his trip to the bathroom; even off duty, Mr Health and Hygiene was inspecting us. And we'd failed. Our house was germ paradise. No wonder Phil wouldn't touch the pie. His dad had probably told him it carried the plague. My stomach twisted as I wheeled the bin through our gate. That was it, then. I doubted the Pardoes would have anything to do with us again, not even if we cleaned the house from top to bottom.

If only I'd been right.

I dragged the bin on to the pavement and went back inside. Mum was in the sitting room watching the news. She smiled and patted the sofa. I shook my head and went upstairs to feed my misery with some maths homework.

I should explain that the news was a big deal

for Mum. For a long time I didn't know why she watched it every night, frowning in concentration, as if waiting – hoping – for something. When it finished she kind of relaxed, but in a droopy way. I remember the day I'd finally understood.

It was a Wednesday morning in April. I was nine. The night before there'd been news of a bush fire in Australia. Flames the colour of egg yolk filled the screen.

'It's not known how the fire started,' said the reporter. Mum gave a little gasp and pressed a hand to her mouth.

The next morning she turned the radio on. We were doing geography, carving a sponge cake in the shape of Australia.

I dipped a piece of shredded wheat in a bowl of red food colouring. 'Where does Ayers Rock go?'

'Shh.' She put a claw to her lips as the news came on.

'With the blaze in Queensland now under control, firefighters say it was caused by an abandoned barbeque. Police have arrested –' She turned off the radio. A tear shushed down her cheek. A flame sprang from her mouth.

I ran to the sink and filled a glass with water. 'What, Mum?'

She gulped it down, quenching the flame. 'It's just . . . I thought maybe . . . oh Aidan, what if there are other fire breathers out there? Whenever there's an unexplained fire, I can't help wondering if it's a cry for contact from another part-dragon.' A thread of smoke curled from her nostril. 'How wonderful,' she said softly, 'not to be alone.'

I felt a nip in my chest. 'You're not. You've got me.'

She stroked my cheek with a claw. 'Course I have.'

But for the first time I glimpsed the deep, empty pot inside her that I couldn't fill. I'd never know how a spark tasted in your mouth or how it felt to shed a scale. I'd never envy bare feet or short sleeves in summer. I'd never feel ashamed of the way I was born.

On Tuesday morning Phil ignored me. At lunchtime, when I went to our usual table, an electric fence of looks sent me packing. He must have told Ben, Dan and Tom I was a health hazard. I found an empty table and sat alone. Until – guess who joined me?

You mean guess who joined *me*? That was my regular spot. And I wasn't happy. Seeing Phil's latest minion in front of me took away my appetite. That and the way you kept staring at my lunch.

Well, you've got to admit it was . . . interesting. One of those silver takeaway boxes with noodles and bits of prawn cracker.

Don't knock leftovers. Dad had bought a Chinese after his shift the night before. A bit slimy but tasty enough. And what about your biscuits? They looked like baked dog poop.

You were quick enough to take a Peawurly (peanut butter and Curly Wurly) cookie when I offered.

I was being polite.

Well, that was a first. And it broke the ice. I said, 'What are you dressing up as on Friday?'

And I said, 'Nothing. I'm not into Halloween.'

I couldn't believe it. 'Don't you like all the sweets and spooky stuff and trick-or-treating?' To be honest, I was trying to sound like an expert. I'd never actually been trick-or-treating. Mum hadn't stopped me. I'd just never been invited. I'd hoped it would be different this year. But the way things were going, I'd be at home bobbing for apples again.

'No I don't,' I said. That was only a third true. Of course I liked the sweets. I'd have loved an invitation to go trick-or-treating too. But the spooky stuff? 'It's boring,' I said. 'Dressing up as vampires and werewolves every single year.'

'So what would you go as?'

'Something Greek. They had the best monsters. Like the Hydra, the snake with nine heads that grew two more if you cut one off. Or Cerberus, the three-headed dog who guarded the entrance to Hades. Or Polyphemus, the Cyclops who — what are you grinning at?'

I couldn't help smiling as I pictured this weeny girl as a giant with one huge eye in her forehead. I managed not to say so, though, and she didn't ask again. She was on a roll.

'— who captured Odysseus in his cave. Or maybe the Sphinx. You'd get to ask all these riddles, and if people couldn't answer them you'd kill them, though maybe I'd just whack them with my paw. Or I'd be a dryad, one of those really shy nymphs who lived in trees. I'd wear a green sheet tied round my waist with ivy, and a headband made of . . .'

She stopped. And she looked at me with big worried eyes, as if she'd suddenly realised how loudly and quickly she was talking, and how she was clenching her fists and leaning forward as if she needed the loo but it would have to wait because there was so much more to tell me.

'Wow,' I said. 'You're into Greek legends, then. And I see what you mean about boring vampires.'

Her mouth spread across her face. I realised that must be a smile, though it vanished soon enough, as if her muscles weren't used to it.

'You want real monsters?' I said. 'Give me your mobile number and I'll send you a link.' Which I did that evening, in my very first text to an actual boy:

Hi Aidan,

www.classicalwisdom.com/top-ten-terrifying-monsters-greek-mythology

Sleep well. If you can.

Charlotte

October 21st

A murmur from Scotland and a whisper from Greece! I can hardly believe it — until I look at Hestia. She gives me faith, not in some fake Father Christmas in the sky but in the genius of Operation Zoe. She's enchanting, miraculous I'd say if I believed in miracles. And if the rumours prove true, I'll soon be putting her talent to the test.

ZOO BLUES

Phil froze me out all week. I ended up chatting to Charlotte most breaks. I knew it didn't look good to hang around with a girl, never mind the class loner. But she was obviously desperate for company.

Excuse me? I'd rather have spent my breaks reading Mycenaean Myths and Monsters but I felt sorry for you.

By Friday, when we broke up for the Halloween mid-term break, even *I* felt sorry for me. I didn't bother dressing up. Phil and Co. were ignoring me completely, apart from sniggering behind their orc masks when they saw me talking to Charlotte.

Mum once told me there are a million words in the English language. But when I got home I didn't feel like using any of them. I went into the kitchen.

She was peeling carrots at the counter. 'Hi, love. Good day?'

I took the milk from the fridge and poured some into a glass.

'Is everything OK?'

I drank the milk.

'Did something happen at school?'

I licked the moustache, cold and silky, from my upper lip.

Mum didn't push but went back to her carrot, slicing off the skin with the tips of her claws. Quiet settled in the kitchen. Nothing but the scrape of claws and the sluggish tick of the clock. *Scrrr. Ctick. Scrrr. Ctick.*

'It's Phil.'

She put the carrot down and came over to the table. Then everything spilled out: how he'd cooled off, cut me out of the group.

'You mean since he visited?' She sat down opposite me.

Yes, I was about to reply, *because his dad thinks we live in a scuzz pit.* But her voice was so soft, and her eyes so scared that she'd failed me again, I found myself saying, 'No, because I've talked to that girl Charlotte. The one he said he hates. She seems lonely.'

'Oh.' Mum nodded, I could tell, with relief. 'Good for you. Why don't you explain to him that you're just being kind? I'm sure he'll understand.'

As if. I was beginning to wonder if 'kind' was one of those million words that Phil hadn't come across.

'Maybe you can help them patch things up,' she said.

Wrong again. I had enough patching up to do myself. And as Phil had done the unpatching, how was I supposed to manage that?

My misery must have shown on my face because she tapped the table with her claws and said brightly, 'Hey, how about the zoo tomorrow? We haven't been for ages.'

We both loved the zoo: me for the ice cream and the chimps, and Mum for the stranger animals. She'd spend ages watching the tapirs with their squirming snouts, like separate creatures stuck to their faces. She loved the mad-eyed sloths and the armour-plated pangolin. Best of all was the star-nosed mole, a cute little furball until you saw its nose like an exploding sea anemone. I think she was comforted by the wild variety of life. It made her feel less of a weirdo.

Maybe that's why I invented recipes too. Maybe hamajamalami (ham, jam and salami) pizzas and Hula Hoop cupcakes are my baking biodiversity: edible versions of the crazy genetic ingredients that make up tapirs, sloths . . . and part-dragons.

Or maybe you just like eating.

Whatever. When we got home from the zoo, I made Crunchie Bar-nana bread to cheer myself up. Mum was chirpy as chips. But I felt sadder than ever. The thought of a week on my own left a hole inside me that even three slices couldn't fill.

'That girl,' Mum said, digging a nugget of chocolate out of a slice of Bar-nana bread with her claw.

'What about her?'

'You could always invite her round.' Mum speared the bean and popped it in her mouth. 'You said she's lonely.'

'And I also said she's a *girl*.' I rolled my eyes. 'Boys don't have *girls* round.'

'Because?'

I wasn't sure why. But I was sure. So I folded my arms. 'No way. OK? Not in a million years.'

I didn't recognise your voice at first. I hadn't bothered looking at the number because the only person who ever phoned was Dad. You didn't even say your name. Just 'Hi, it's me,' as if I must have been sitting there all weekend waiting for you to call. By the time I remembered who had my number, from the monster link I'd sent, you were gabbling something down the phone. I didn't catch a word. So you ended up inviting me twice. Ha, how keen is that?

October 26th

What a week. The news from Scotland and Greece looks more and more promising. And even better, I might have my first hard evidence, found here in Ireland of all places. Tests so far have confirmed nothing, which could tell me everything. All the results — chemical composition, hardness and heat conductivity — suggest a substance unknown to science. That makes complete sense if these little beauties on my desk are what I hope.

But hope mustn't cloud my judgement. Like any true scientist, I'll continue testing to prove what they're not.

HELP!

How was I supposed to entertain a girl? Football was obviously out. It was lashing rain on Monday so a walk was out too. The X-box was probably out; Charlotte didn't seem like a screeny sort of person. Her lunch, her shoes, the way she walked – there was something unsophisticated about her.

What's that supposed to mean?!

It's a compliment. I thought you'd know that. 'Sophisticated' comes from a Greek word meaning to cheat or deceive.

Like Phil, you mean?

I guess so. You were unsoPhilsticated.

Ha slightly funny ha. Go on.

But there was one thing that Charlotte loved, and another thing that I loved. Put them together and what did you get? A good hour of Googling and a fair bit of shopping on Monday morning.

I was in the sitting room when the bell rang

at three o'clock. I waited eleven seconds before getting up.

You counted?

I didn't want to look too keen. But I did want to see your parents. I couldn't imagine what they'd be like. Actually, I know it sounds stupid, but I couldn't imagine you *having* parents. Definitely not brothers or sisters. You're kind of a one-off.

Right about the siblings, half-right about the parents. Mum went off with the dentist when I was seven.

I was too late. When I opened the door, the one remaining parent was driving off in his taxi. Charlotte stood on the doorstep with wide, worried eyes. She was gripping a DVD with both hands. '*Hercules.*'

For some reason her nervousness made me relax. 'Thanks. We can watch it later. Come in.' I took her coat and led her down the hall to the kitchen.

Mum was at the sink washing grapes. She turned and smiled. 'Hi Charlotte. Nice to meet you. I'm Shauna. Aidan's told me lots about you.'

I glared at her. Clever, nice and unpopular was hardly lots.

'Eczema,' I blurted out, pointing to Mum's gloves. After Phil's visit, I wanted to get it over with.

I waited for the scrunched nose and awkward questions. All I got was 'Oh.'

Mum brought the grapes to the table. 'I like your

hair,' she said. 'I've always wanted curls.' Cringe.

But Charlotte gave one of her rare smiles. 'Well, I've always wanted straight hair.'

Mum laughed. 'We should swap.' She added the grapes to a basket of fruit, next to a jar of honey and a pot of Greek yoghurt. 'I'll leave you to it.'

I wasn't even looking at Charlotte, but I could feel the air go stiff around her. She felt as awkward being left together as I did. 'Actually, Mum, could you help us get started?'

'On what?' Charlotte said.

Mum explained. I was about to add, 'It's just an idea. We can do something else if you want.' But when I saw Charlotte's face I didn't bother.

'You mean we can use any of this?' She pointed at the table. Mum nodded.

'Amazing.' Charlotte shook her head in wonder. 'Except.' She frowned. 'All I know is that ambrosia was the food of the gods. No one knows what was in it.'

'That's the point,' I said. 'We'll invent our own ambrosia.'

Charlotte stared at the fruit bowl. 'I've never even *seen* half these things. Is that a pomegranate?' She pointed to a round red fruit with a star-shaped knob at the top.

Then I told you the story of Persephone, the girl who was skipping round the Greek countryside when King Hades appeared and whisked her down to the underworld.

Above the ground her mum, Demeter, goddess of the harvest, stopped all green things from growing. Zeus, the chief god, ordered Persephone's release. Hades said OK but he fed her six pomegranate seeds. That was a trick, as anyone who ate or drank in the underworld would have to return. So while Persephone comes back to earth every spring, she has to go underground every winter to be Hades' wife. Bummer.

Aidan's Amazing Ambrosia
Hey, it was Charlotte's too.
But that doesn't start with A.
So let's go halves.
Aidotte's Amazing Ambrosia
Ten grapes
Seeds of one pomegranate
Two tablespoons of honey
Half a cup of Greek yoghurt
Put everything in a liquidiser.
And whizz up a divine smoothie.

I poured the pink goo into three glasses. We all took a sip. Sweet and creamy with a pippy crunch, it really was fit for the gods.

Charlotte licked froth from her lips. 'No wonder the Greeks thought it made you immortal.'

I drained my cup. 'Does that mean we'll live forever now?'

'I hope not,' Mum said. 'Boring.'

'Not if we drank this every day,' said Charlotte. 'Can we make something else?'

We spent the whole afternoon cooking. Well, to be accurate, Mum and I cooked while Charlotte told us stories about the gods. The things they got up to – sneaking, flirting and fighting – it was Ancient Greek *Hollyoaks*.

Charlotte was livelier than I'd ever seen her. At school she walked about like a fist on legs, tight and bunched and ready to punch. But now, as we listened and laughed, she seemed to uncurl and settle into herself. Her eyes lost their hunted look, her mouth found new muscles to smile with. I'd never seen Mum drop her guard so much with a stranger either. And I'd never come so close to forgetting what she had to guard.

At dinner we sat down to a Greek feast. For starters, pita bread and home-made tzatziki. The main course was moussaka and Greek salad, followed by a dessert of Greek yoghurt with pomegranate sauce.

Mum pushed her chair back. 'If that's how the Ancient Greeks ate, no wonder they needed the Olympic Games to burn it off.' She held her stomach.

'Actually,' said Charlotte, 'the Olympics were invented for the gods. One story is that five brothers raced at Olympia to entertain the baby Zeus. Another one says that Zeus's son Hercules started the games.'

'You're a walking encyclopaedia,' Mum said. 'Is there anything you don't know?'

Charlotte went pomegranate-red. She paused for a second too long.

Well, it was a hard question. I know more than most of the class about most subjects.

Except one. Modesty.

Modesty means not boasting. And I'm not, I'm just telling the truth. Anyway, I did think of something. 'Cooking,' I said. 'I've learned loads this afternoon. My dad's useless in the kitchen.'

'Why don't you come again?' Mum said. 'Aidan can teach you some basic meals.'

Wow, I thought, shooting her a look from Mordor. Thanks for asking me first.

'Wow,' I said. 'I'd love to.'

October 28th

Still running tests on those Irish samples, and awaiting confirmation of the subjects from Greece and Scotland. Meantime I'll interview the nurses who answered my advert in the local paper. If everything works out, I'll soon be welcoming my first guests. Awesome.

MID-TERM BAKE

It's not that I hadn't enjoyed Charlotte's visit. I really had. It was just that the more we became friends, the harder things would be with Phil. But there were still six days before school. I might as well have company and worry about him next week.

On Tuesday afternoon I finally met her dad. He was standing behind her when I opened the door. 'You must be Aidan. I'm Charlotte's . . .' He put his hands on her shoulders. 'Well, obviously.' He smiled shyly. He had a soft, baggy face and mini versions of her brown eyes. 'You're very good to have her over again.'

There were droopy lines round his mouth that made me want to cheer him up. 'Pleasure,' I said, trying to sound warm and cool at the same time.

'Well, I do appreciate it.' He shuffled from one foot to the other. 'I'm on the late shift so it's grand to know she's got company.' He kissed the top of her head. 'See you at eight, Charlie.'

'Don't *call* me that,' she muttered, scowling for Ireland.

'Charlie?' I said, closing the door. '*Charlie?*' She looked at me. And I have never.

Ever.

Said.

It.

Again.

Mum and I had spent the morning shopping for basic meals to teach her over the week. I started with spaghetti bolognese. I showed her how to chop an onion without crying (put it in the freezer fifteen minutes beforehand) and how to crush garlic with a fork. When the meat had browned, I told her to choose a new ingredient to make it her own special recipe.

Grape-etti bolognese. Hmm. Three out of ten.

On Wednesday I taught her to roast a chicken. Her special ingredient: a layer of strawberry jam over the skin before cooking. Four out of ten for appearance (alarmingly sunburnt) and five for taste (disturbingly sweet).

Thursday was stir-fry chicken. I gave instructions and Charlotte did all the work, chopping vegetables, frying them with chicken and adding her special ingredient.

Wine gums.

Once they'd melted properly, an amazing eight out of ten.

Friday was Halloween. Mum made a witchy stew of beef and vegetables, and Charlotte added a spooky extra.

Human fingers, aka fun-size bananas.

As for dessert – well, that was my department. It's a family tradition. Every Halloween I cook up a creepy surprise. Three years ago it was glow-in-the-dark icing. Two years ago I made chocolate cupcake vampire bats that hung upside down from the ceiling on black thread. Last year it was a mutant spider cake with blood sauce. This year's offering was round and white. Charlotte and Mum sat at the kitchen table while I brought it out of the fridge on a plate.

'Ghost cake,' I announced, putting it on the table. It was covered in roll-on icing, draped to look like a sheet. There were two red holes for eyes, made from hollowed-out strawberries. Their pointy ends stuck down into the cake. Mum clapped.

'Brilliant,' said Charlotte.

'Not yet.' I reached up to a shelf and brought down the bottle of brandy that we used every Christmas to make brandy butter icing for the cake. I poured some into a cup, put it in the microwave and turned it on.

'What are you doing, Aidan?' Mum stood up from her chair. 'You can't have alcohol.'

'It's not for drinking.' I grinned and fetched a matchbox from the counter. I took the cup of warmed brandy from the microwave and dribbled some into each hollow strawberry. Then I picked up the matchbox and struck a match. It scraped uselessly against the side of the box. I tried another. Same thing. 'Come on!' I muttered.

The third match hissed into flame. I dipped it into the brandy-filled strawberry. 'Ow!' The flame scorched my fingertip. I blew it out. 'It's too deep,' I said, taking another match. 'The brandy's meant to catch fire, but I can't reach –'

A flame sprang from each cakey eye.

'Ta-daah!' Mum sang.

My heart punched into my head. I dropped the matchbox. And Charlotte . . .

Screamed. I shoved my chair back and jumped up. Mrs Mooney looked at me with terrified eyes. Then she ran out of the kitchen.

I pressed my hands to my cheeks. 'How did she . . . do that?'

Aidan stared at me. 'Do what?' he said in a tiny voice.

I swallowed. 'Light the cake.'

'Wha—?' His mouth froze into an O. Then he said, 'It was me. I lit the match and —'

'No you didn't.' I took a step backwards. 'Mrs Mooney

breathed on it. I saw a flame come . . .' I pressed my hand against the cool, sensible wall. 'From her mouth.'

'Oh,' Aidan said faintly. 'That. OK. Yeah. It's a trick.' He coughed. 'Mum used to do this act. On the street. You know, where they swallow lighter fuel.'

'She didn't swallow anything.' I pressed my lips together.

'Didn't you see her take that sip of brandy?'

I shook my head.

'Well, she did. Obviously.' His voice was loud now. 'How else would she get a flame?'

I backed into the doorway. 'I don't know. But she didn't drink anything.'

'Yes she did.' There was a kind of begging in Aidan's eyes, as if he was desperate for me to stop. 'I told you, it's a trick.'

'So why was she upset? Why did she run out?'

Aidan pulled out a chair from the table and sort of flopped into it. 'The thing is,' he said slowly, 'she shouldn't have done it. It's dangerous.'

I took a step towards the table. 'Why?'

'There was an accident. Ages ago.' He cleared his throat. 'She was doing her act on the street. A man in the audience came forward to see how she did it.' He chewed the edge of his lip. 'And the flame from her mouth caught his jacket. The collar.'

I perched on the edge of a chair.

'Luckily there was a fire extinguisher. So the man wasn't hurt. But Mum got such a fright, she gave up the act.' He leaned towards me. 'So please don't tell anyone. It would just upset her more.' He clasped his hands together on the table. 'And she could get into trouble.' His fingers twisted together. 'If the police found out. So don't even tell your dad. OK?'

I nodded. What else could I do?

Aidan smiled really, really brightly. 'Want some cake?'

What could I do but nod again?

He fetched a knife and cut ghostly slices, gabbling on about nothing. But it was no good. Fear had flown into the room. It sat between us like an injured bird, trapped and trembling. For the first time that week I couldn't wait for the doorbell.

When it rang, I jumped up. 'Thanks then. Bye.'

Aidan followed me into the hall. 'Not even your dad,' he said, taking my coat off the banister. 'Promise?'

'Promise.'

'How do I know you mean it?'

I could have said, 'Because my dad might freak and not let me come again, which would be the worst thing ever.' I could have said, 'Because I don't care if your mum does dangerous tricks, she's still great.' But I didn't. 'Because,' I said, snatching my coat, 'I promised. And if you don't trust me, you can go and boil your butt.'

I walked to the car in silence.

'Had fun?' said Dad as we drove off.

'Mmm.'

'What was tonight's dinner?'

I told him.

'Very spooky.' He gave what was meant to be a witchy

cackle but sounded more like a problem with the engine. 'And dessert?'

I turned away so he wouldn't see my face. 'A cake.' I stared through the window at the halos of street lamps, fuzzy as dreams, and tried to make sense of what I'd seen.

Not a lighted match, that's for sure. And definitely not one single sip of brandy.

STORY TIME

The minute Charlotte had gone, I ran upstairs to Mum's bedroom. She was sitting on the bed with her legs drawn up and her arms wrapped around them. Her gloves were on the bedside table beside an empty glass.

She looked up. Her cheeks were red and scratched, like grazed knees. 'What have I done?'

I'd been ready to blame her, to bawl her out. But seeing her there, hugging her knees like a lost little girl, I said instead, 'It's my fault. For making that cake.' I came over and sat on the edge of the bed. 'I made up a story.' My throat was thick. I forced my voice through and told her about the street act gone wrong.

Mum pressed a claw to her mouth. 'Did she believe it?'

'Pretty much.' I tried to smile but only my grimace muscles were working. Because even if that was true – which I doubted – 'pretty much' wasn't enough. Charlotte was bound to ask more questions. And we'd have to answer them all.

Or rather I would. Mum had just had the shock of her life. I needed to keep her as calm as possible, which also meant out of the way. 'I'll invite Charlotte round to cook again, like it's no big deal. If she brings it up, I'll repeat the story. The more she hears it, the more she'll forget what she saw.'

'A woman breathing fire without matches or fuel?' Mum closed her eyes. 'Pretty hard to forget, don't you think?'

'But even harder to believe. Harder than a street act. I'll pad the story out, make it totally believable.'

'What about her dad?' Mum said. 'She's probably telling him right now.'

'She promised she wouldn't,' I said. And from the way Charlotte's eyes had bored into me, I believed her. I had to. Because the alternative was too huge to fit in my head.

I spent the next hour Googling everything I could about street-performing fire-breathers. The fuel (paraffin), the torch (metal with a cotton wick), the dangers (flames in your face, stomach ulcers). Then I practised the story with enough detail to make it convincing but not confusing (the man's name was Gary Shaw, his jacket was denim, Mum gave him money for another one).

Well, I was Googling too. And I ended up more confused than ever.

October 31st

Brilliant news all round! First, Scotland and Greece are on. Second, I've run every test there is and am sure the samples are new to science. And finally, I've found the perfect nurse: strong and surly as hell with a small, tight mouth that looks like it won't spill too many beans. She'll need a few days to settle in — and then we're in business.

MAKE-BELIEVE

It should have been funny. We were using fiction to explain a fact that the whole world thought was fiction. But I wasn't laughing when I texted Charlotte next morning. I had to convince her. Mum's future – *my* future – depended on it. My fingers shook as I pressed my phone.

Wanto come at 11 & nake lasagme?

The answer came five seconds later.

Yes

I decided I'd take Charlotte into the kitchen and start cooking. I'd give her lots of jobs to do: fetching ingredients, chopping, peeling. When she brought up the fire-breathing – which I knew she would – I'd repeat the street story, in between giving orders, so that she'd only half-concentrate. Mum would poke her head round the door, normal as pie, then go off again. It seemed a good plan.

But Charlotte had a different one. When I

opened the door, she marched past me. 'Where's your mum?' she said, looking round the hall.

Lies queued up in my head. *In the shower. Mind your own business. Dunno.* But in my head they stayed. 'Upstairs,' I heard myself say. Dammit.

'I need to talk to her.'

Again my brain came up with options: *She's busy, She's ill* or just plain *No.* But again my voice had a mind of its own. 'Mu-u-m,' it called upstairs. My heart was doing press-ups.

She appeared on the landing. 'Hi.' Her smile was thin and bright.

Charlotte climbed two stairs. She stopped. 'The thing is.' She climbed two more and stopped again, looking from Mum to me and back. 'I went home last night and Googled fire-breathing. And Googled and Googled. I couldn't find any way of doing it without putting fuel in your mouth first and having a spark to light it.' She blinked at Mum. 'I never saw you drink brandy and I didn't see a match light up before you breathed on the cake.' She swallowed. 'So you need to tell me how you did it.' Her voice was getting faster. 'There are three possible ways. One: I missed it, in which case you can do it again right now. Two: you did it another way that isn't on the internet, and which you can – you *must* – show me. Or three,' she took a deep breath, 'the craziest way of all, which kind of makes sense because it would explain why Aidan's been homeschooled and why you wear gloves and hide away, and in another way makes no sense at all because there's no such thing as –' she caught her breath – 'dragons.'

There was a noise in my head like the Tardis taking off. I grabbed the banister. Or maybe it grabbed me.

'At least,' Charlotte went on, 'people *say* dragons aren't real but there are photos of yeti footprints and the Loch Ness Monster, so maybe the truth about some things gets all tangled up. And to be honest it would be totally weird, and I *was* totally weirded out last night, but it would also be fantastic and incredible, though not incredible as in unbelievable because, if it's true, then I have to believe it. Plus, I've had a few hours to get used to the idea and now I think it would be the most brilliant thing ever, so please tell me I'm right.'

Mum stood there, pale and still and apparently not breathing.

Charlotte was off again. 'Because the thing is, I thought about the Ancient Greeks and how they believed in mythical creatures as if they were real, like gorgons and the Cyclops and the Minotaur and don't get me going on all the gods. And some of the creatures were *partly* real and *partly* mythical, like centaurs which were half-people and half-horses, and fauns which were man-goats, so why couldn't you have some dragony bits, like your hands, for instance, which is why you wear gloves?'

I gasped. Mum looked down at her gloved hands, hanging by her sides.

'And if I'm right,' Charlotte squeaked on, 'you need to know that it's OK, I understand why you want to keep it secret because you can't trust anyone except me, and I won't tell a soul because, number one, I thought you were fantastic *before* last night and I think you're even more fantastic now, which means that, number two, I'm not scared of you and, number three, I'm not going to lose the new and actually *only* friends I've got by blabbing their secret, and now I've answered your questions, you've got to answer mine. Am I right?' She stood on the stairs, her hand on the banister and her face all scrunched with excitement, though, being Charlotte, it looked more like anger.

I waited for the blush, the sweat, the rush to the bathroom and slam of the door. But instead Mum did something far more terrifying, dangerous and – let's face it – insane. She smiled.

We sat at the kitchen table eating ghost cake. It seemed fitting to finish the food that had started the trouble.

'A *real* dragon?' Charlotte's eyes were as round as coins.

Mum nodded. 'Completely real. Though not complete.' She put her left hand on the table, palm down. 'You guessed right.' She caught the middle finger of her glove and pulled it slowly.

Charlotte squealed. I pressed a fist to my mouth to hold back the anger bubbling inside. How *dare* Mum? She'd kept me at home all these years to protect her secret, and now, just a few weeks into school, *she* was the one sharing it!

'Scales,' Charlotte whispered. She lifted her hand as if in a dream. Gazing at Mum, she crooked her forefinger. Mum nodded. Charlotte reached across the table. Her hand hovered over Mum's claw. She stuck out her forefinger, tapped a scale and drew it back, quick as a hen peck. 'Wow,' she breathed. 'Just wow.'

Mum smiled. Pulling off her other glove, she spread her hands on the table. Charlotte put a finger on Mum's right wrist and ran it along the back of her hand to the base of a claw. 'They're so beautiful.'

My knuckles were hurting. I realised my teeth were stuck in them. I dropped my fist as Charlotte's questions flew. 'Are your feet scaly too? Can you fly? Do you have a tail?'

I listened in silence. After her outburst on the

stairs, you'd think I'd have weighed in, told her she was talking nonsense and hammered home the street act story. But Mum's smile had said it all. What was the point of pretending?

'Are you cold-blooded? Do you have dragon parents? Do you have *any* parents?'

As Mum answered, the knot in my chest began to loosen. This was her secret, not mine. She had the right to hide it or share it with anyone she chose. And, wonder of wonders, look who she *had* chosen: a cross little person with great big eyes and looney-tune hair.

'Did you hatch from an egg? How *do* you breathe fire?'

'I don't know,' Mum said. She explained that, with doctors and dentists out of bounds, there was no way of examining her anatomy. 'But we have a theory about my fuel source.'

I told her about farts, or the lack of them.

Charlotte nodded. 'Makes sense. I read that humans can produce two litres of gas every day.' She looked so solemn I couldn't help smiling. There wasn't a flicker of fear or disgust in her eyes. More questions crowded on her face, creasing her forehead, pursing her mouth. She settled on one and turned to me. 'Do you have dragon parts too?'

Looking into those hopeful eyes, I almost wanted to lie. But I didn't.

'At least,' Mum said, 'nothing that shows. But who knows what Aidan carries inside him?'

Charlotte frowned. 'What do you mean?'

'My DNA.' I explained about genes that could hide for generations.

'Wow.' Charlotte blinked. 'So once upon a time, dragons walked the earth. Imagine!' She gave a little shiver. 'I'm glad I wasn't around. It must have been terrifying. Oh –'

The minute I said it, I realised how it must sound. I put a hand to my mouth. 'I'm sorry, Mrs Mooney. No offence.'

She smiled. 'None taken.'

Not by her, at least, who had reason to. But someone else took a bucket-load.

THE TRUTH ABOUT DRAGONS

Well, it's my truth, anyway. A different truth, a possible truth, because the real truth is that no one *knows* the truth. And when I smacked the table and snapped at Charlotte, 'Why does everyone hate them?' it's because I was sick of the way people swallow the stories, from St George to *The Hobbit*, without questioning them.

My version – the one I'd come up with after years of struggling to fit the mother I knew to the monsters I read about – made more sense. And now that Charlotte knew about Mum, it was time to knock her prejudice on its Smaugy little head. 'Perhaps we all come from dragons,' I said. 'Perhaps they're a missing link in evolution.'

'What?!' Charlotte's eyebrows leapt above her glasses. Then they dropped and bunched together. 'So why don't we all have dragon parts?'

'Perhaps we do but they're hidden. Or perhaps we did ages ago, and the genes only survived in a few people. And once in a thousand years or so, they pop out.'

'But what about fossils? Why has no one ever found one of a dragon?'

I shrugged. 'Maybe there aren't any. Maybe acid from the gas inside them dissolved their bones or something.'

'But that's just a crazy guess. There's not one bit of proof it's true.'

I folded my arms. 'And there's not one bit of proof it isn't. Either way, it's a good story. Do you want to hear it or not?'

She nodded. Her curls bounced like excited earthworms.

'You know how scientists say that some apes evolved into humans and others stayed as apes? Well, maybe the same went for dragons, only further back in evolution. And maybe the ones that stayed as dragons lived alongside humans.'

'Wow,' Charlotte breathed. Her eyes were so full of wonder that I dropped the 'maybe'.

'Dragons were gentle animals,' I said. 'Cavemen tamed some of them and used their fire. Others were hunted for food. They got scared and went to live in lonely places. But show-offy knights wouldn't leave them alone. They went on quests to kill dragons and impress princesses. The dragons got fed up. A few of them attacked villages. That gave knights a proper excuse to hunt them. When they went extinct, though, everyone felt guilty. So people started telling each other that dragons had never really existed. They turned them into fiction and hyped up the bad bits. And now, after hundreds of years, humans have actually forgotten that dragons were ever real.'

'Except us.' Charlotte's eyes shone. I swear there were tears in them.

'And only us,' Mum said. 'If anyone else found out . . .' She shook her head.

'It's OK, Mrs Mooney,' said Charlotte. 'I get it. I mean, I don't get what it's like to have those.' She reached across the table and laid her hand on Mum's claws. 'But I get what it's like to be different. To feel like you never fit in, that you're always on the outside. To be so lonely your teeth hurt.' She pushed her glasses up her nose. 'That's why you can trust me. I've just had the best week in, like, forever. So I'm hardly going to ruin everything by telling your secret. To anyone. Ever. Including my dad. Cross my heart.'

I put my hand on my chest. Mrs Mooney smiled. I could tell she believed me. Maybe it takes an outsider to trust an outsider. Aidan was trying to smile too but there were two vertical lines between his eyebrows like the marks on a pause button. I didn't blame him. I could promise and swear, cross my heart till I died, but what was the point?

Only one thing would prove I could keep their secret. And that was to keep their secret.

That afternoon Charlotte begged for some dragony action. She started small. 'Can you peel an apple with your claw, Mrs Mooney?' Mum carved the skin off in a single spiral.

'Cool. Can you light a candle?'

There was one in a glass on the kitchen window sill. Mum breathed gently on the wick. A flame sprang up.

'Brilliant,' Charlotte said as the smell of cinnamon filled the air. 'What about boiling a pot of water?'

'She can do better than that,' I said, fetching a metal teapot from the counter. I dropped two teabags inside and put the pot in the sink.

Mum stood over it and breathed, moving her head to train the flame evenly round the pot. After a minute or so she stopped. I took a cloth, lifted the pot and poured its contents into a mug.

Charlotte sipped the steaming tea. 'Fantastic!'

Best of all was lighting the fire in the sitting room. Mum knelt in front of the hearth. She puffed out her cheeks and blew hard. A jet of flame hit the pyramid of twigs and newspaper in the grate.

'Genius,' Charlotte whispered as the kindling crackled and spat.

Mum sat back on her heels. 'Hardly. It's just a puff of air.'

'But the flame's different every time. For the candle it was small and yellow. For the teapot it was all blue and feathery. And this one was like a laser beam, thin and solid. You're like a painter mixing the right colour, or a violinist finding the perfect note.'

Mum laughed. 'I'd never thought of it like that. You're very kind.' She stood up. 'But to be honest, I've spent my life wishing I didn't have this . . . thing.'

'Well, I wish I didn't have this.' Charlotte scrunched a handful of hair. 'Or these.' She tapped her glasses. 'Or squeaky old this.' She patted her mouth, which I guess meant her voice. 'At least *your* thing is useful.'

'How?' Mum sighed. Smoke coiled from her nostrils like the ghosts of pencil shavings. 'A few silly tricks maybe. But only inside these walls.' She wiggled her claws. 'And these? What use are they?'

'They're beautiful,' Charlotte said firmly, 'which is its own kind of useful.'

Mum had no answer for that. Smiling, she went out.

Charlotte gazed at the fire. 'Amazing,' she murmured. 'You must be so proud of her.'

'What?' I stared at her. I'd felt lots of things about Mum. Angry, embarrassed, sorry-for. But proud?

Charlotte stared back. 'Well, I would be.' Her eyes drilled a hole in my face. 'I wish she was my mum.'

I felt a sting of shame, as if she'd stubbed out a cigarette in my chest.

November 3rd

My first two guests have arrived. Confused and scared as hell, of course. But now I've explained, they're coming round and starting to see what a privilege this is, what a gift to the world.

Wish I could fetch the last guest myself, but my work's cut out for me here. I'll tell Derek to minimise the talk. It could be a bumpy ride.

And a busy few days, too. I'll have to take a rain check on the diary.

TROY STORY

Our worst fear had come true. Mum's secret was out. And guess what? It brought a strange relief, as if a blister swollen with years of dread had finally burst. At last there was someone I could relax with outside the family without worrying that Mum's glove might slip or a flame sneak out.

It also brought a problem, though. School. Being friends with Charlotte would hardly win me cool points with anyone, never mind Phil. But I had no choice. If I upset her, she could leak our secret.

So that's why on Monday you invited me round again.

No. Well, maybe a teeny bit.

Wow, thanks.

But at break, when Phil was ruder than ever, I was totally glad you were coming. I was in the yard, offering round mystery muffins.*

'Poison,' he said loudly as he walked past.

---

* I figured the mystery ingredient might put them off. But Susie was right. The recipe's on page 256.

Never mind him. I heard Susie Costello telling Claire Farrell they were delicious. And Conor Murphy took three.

Charlotte's rucksack was bulging when we walked home on Wednesday. I thought it was just her usual stack of books until Mum opened the door.

'Hi, Mrs Mooney.' She dumped her rucksack in the hall. 'I brought you a present.' She opened the top. 'To thank you for having me round so much.'

'How lovely,' Mum said, hugging her.

Charlotte pulled out a small cardboard box stuck to a bigger one. The small box had a paper triangle each side. Four straws poked down from the bigger box.

Lovely wasn't quite the word. Mum tried again. 'How . . . original.'

'It should have wheels.'

'Oh.' Mum looked even more baffled. 'Right.'

Charlotte took it into the kitchen and stood it on the table. She motioned for us to sit down.

'For ten years,' she said, 'the Greeks besieged the city of Troy. They wanted to rescue Queen Helen but they couldn't get over the city wall. At last Odysseus came up with a plan.'

'So that's what it's meant to be.' I laughed. 'The wooden horse of Troy. You could've fooled me.'

Charlotte sniffed. 'Well, it fooled the Trojans. The Greeks left the horse at the city gates and hid round the corner, pretending they'd gone home. The Trojans thought it was a present. They opened the gates, wheeled the horse inside and ...' she put her hand under the lower box and pulled down a flap, 'out jumped the Greek soldiers.' Five tiny gingerbread men dropped on to the table.

Mum clapped. 'Brilliant!'

'I looked up the recipe for gingerbread,' Charlotte said proudly.

'What a great idea.' And being Mum, it led to another one. Two hours later we'd baked and built the gingerbread city of Troy, complete with houses, people and surrounding wall. We stood the cooled buildings and citizens on a tray, stuck down with icing. Our Troy-on-a-Tray was perfect. The walls looked like sandstone and the people had a lovely ginger tan. Charlotte had given one of them a long robe and a pointing arm. 'That's Cassandra,' she said, 'the priestess who warned the Trojans not to let the horse in.'

Mum put Troy-on-a-tray in the oven. It came out perfectly. The walls looked like sandstone and the citizens had a lovely ginger tan.

I was just about to nibble King Priam when Mum said, 'Why don't you take this into school tomorrow? What a great way of teaching the story – to eat it.'

I wrinkled my nose. 'I dunno. It's OK for homeschool but . . .' I remembered my first morning and the biodiversity disaster. 'It's a bit –'

Before I could say 'nerdy', Charlotte burst out, 'Brilliant!'

And that was that. When it comes to Greek legends, you don't mess with Charlotte.

Next morning Miss Burkitt loved it, Charlotte retold it and the class ate it.

'Deadly,' Conor Murphy said, chewing Paris, Prince of Troy.

Claire Farrell rescued Helen from the palace tower. 'Safe at last, Queenie,' she said, and bit her head off.

Only Phil and gang refused. When I offered them some Trojan wall, he gave me the oddest look: a mixture of anger, envy and what looked amazingly like fear.

Because for once he wasn't the centre of attention — or so I thought. People were crowding round *us*. Kennedy said it was the best lesson ever. Andy Dunne told me I was a great storyteller. That was the first time he'd spoken to me all term.

Miss Burkitt called us up at the end. 'Charlotte and Aidan,' she said, 'that was wonderful.' Everyone clapped. 'Please bake us another legend.'

THE HEDGE

We decided on a gorgon cake. I knew Mum would be fine with me inviting Charlotte round after school. We stopped at the Spar. I bought strawberry laces for the monster's snakey hair, and glacier mints for her deadly eyes that turned people to stone.

I rang the doorbell. When Mum didn't come, I took out my key. 'Hi,' I called, opening the door. No answer. 'Mum?' I called up the stairs.

'Maybe she's out the back,' said Charlotte.

I went to the kitchen. There was a pile of dirty plates in the sink. I opened the back door. 'Mu–hum!' She wasn't in the garden.

Or the sitting room. I went upstairs. The bedrooms and bathroom were empty.

So was the bathroom in the hall.

I came downstairs and opened the front door. The car was in the drive. 'I'll try the garage.'

The next few minutes are tangled kite strings in my memory. Across the front lawn, I caught sight of the hedge. There was a gash of brown twigs at the top amid the green leaves. I saw the gate too. The tops of the wooden posts were black. On the driveway beneath it, glistening in the sunshine, lay two rainbow drops of oil.

Not oil. Scales.

My heart slammed into my ribs. My legs gave way. I sat on the drive and put my head between my knees.

'Aidan?'

I looked up. Charlotte stood over me. 'What's the matter?' she said.

I pointed to the hedge, the gate, the scales.

I covered my mouth to hold in the scream.

The next thing I remember is sitting on the bottom stair. There was no point checking round the house again. We'd seen enough to know that Mum hadn't left by choice. The loose scales – which Charlotte must have rescued from the path because they now sat gleaming on her palm – the burnt hedge and gatepost, all spoke of struggle. Outside, in full view! My chest filled with ice. Someone must have seen her breathe fire: at the very least the person she'd fought, if not the whole neighbourhood walking its dog or watering its garden.

'Where's your phone?' Charlotte said. I pointed to my schoolbag. She passed it to me. I don't know how my fingers stayed still enough to press Mum's number.

The ringtone came from the sitting room.

I ended the call. 'She left it here.' I closed my eyes. We sat in silence.

A terrible thought slipped into my mind, like a looter through the wreckage of a plane. I opened my eyes. 'You didn't . . . ?'

Charlotte frowned. 'Didn't what?' Then she gasped. 'Are you for real?' She jumped up. 'How could you *possibly* think,' she whispered, shaking her head, 'that I would ever breathe *one word* to *anyone* about your mum?' There were tears in her eyes.

'It's just,' I swallowed, 'she's been safe all her life. Then you found out last week. And now this.'

Charlotte crouched in front of me. 'I know. It's a horrible, dreadful coincidence. But that's exactly what it is. I swear I haven't said a thing.' She caught my arm. 'You've got to believe me.' Her eyes were huge and still.

'I – I'm sorry,' I mumbled. 'Not thinking straight.'

I obviously wasn't either because next thing I knew I was hugging him. 'We should check the house again. But don't touch anything. There might be fingerprints for the gardaí.'

'*Gardaí?*' I sat back and gave a harsh laugh-that-wasn't. 'You think we can report a missing dragon?'

'They won't know,' Charlotte said, 'if we don't tell them.'

'But whoever took Mum must have seen her set fire to the hedge. If the guards catch the person, they'll find out about her soon enough.'

'So? Surely it's not a crime to be part-dragon.'

I not-laughed again. 'I don't suppose so. But I bet there's no law against the guards telling the press, either. And then what?' I could only imagine. Cameras at the window, reporters on the lawn, hot-dog stands on the street, scientists and science fiction writers on TV, politicians and psychologists, a tweeting, snapchatting, instagramming, facebooking explosion. Goodbye school, goodbye home, goodbye Mum. Social services would send me to live with Nando and Gramps on the grounds of fire risk or mythological special needs. And much as I love my grandparents, it hit me like a hurley in the chest that there was no one I could bear to live with except my scaly-handed, claw-fingered, non-farting, fire-breathing mum. And now she'd gone.

Tears fizzed at the back of my eyes. No way could I let Charlotte see me cry. I stood up. 'Thanks for coming,' I said like an idiot. 'I'll phone you later.'

I wasn't offended. I understood he needed space.

I took my phone from my bag. 'What'll I tell my dad?'

'Nothing. Not one single thing. You understand?' He said it so fiercely that I had to nod, though I wasn't sure I agreed. This was too big for us. We needed some grown-up help. On the other hand, what could Dad do except call the guards? And Aidan was right — that could be the worst thing ever for Mrs Mooney.

I phoned Dad in the hall, put on my chirpiest voice and asked him to collect me. I let myself out and walked down the drive, turning my head from the terrible hole that had ripped through the hedge and our world.

BESIDE MYSELF

It sounds physically impossible, but that's how I felt after Charlotte left, bursting with such a dreadful energy that it felt like there were two of me. I ran up the stairs, two at a time, and scoured the bedrooms and bathroom. I ran down again and rechecked all the rooms, the drawers, the cupboards and shelves, then the garden, the car and the garage. Nothing. No scribbled notes or strange objects. I went into the kitchen and sat at the table. I put my head in my hands and had an actual, proper cry. After a bit I felt calmer, as if the panic was leaking away down my face. So, in another impossible move, I pulled myself together. 'Mum might be fine,' I said out loud. I got up and went to the fridge to find something for dinner. 'Maybe she'll phone.'

Of course she wasn't fine. Of course she'd have phoned already. I shut the fridge door. How could I think of food? I took a notepad and pen from a drawer and went into the sitting room. I had to focus, come up with a plan.

After half an hour I'd written two columns:

Action	Problem
Go and look for her	Where?
Tell Nando and Gramps	They could have heart attacks
Put a Missing Person photo in shop windows	1. Pointless if she's been kidnapped and hidden away 2. Dangerous if she and her dragon-ness are discovered
Wait for kidnapper(s) to phone	*I'll* have a heart attack waiting

Not an encouraging list. I chewed my pen. Then I grabbed the remote and switched on the TV.

Anything to fill the silence, to push out the questions crowding my mind. *Where is she? Who took her? Why? What if she's . . . ?*

I turned the volume up super-loud and sat like a zombie. There was a programme about ships, or maybe it was pianos. The news came on. I didn't notice who the presenter was, or what she or he was wearing. I didn't follow the top story or the second one. I couldn't tell you who was protesting about what in Cork, or was it Limerick? But I *can* tell you what came next. A yell. From me.

I took the pen and paper and scribbled madly. When the report had finished, I read over my notes. My heart was jumping like popcorn in a pan.

> Fire at government building,
> Gilligoole Mountains, Co. Galway –
> International Research Centre – no
> injuries – local firemen say cause
> unknown.

Could it be her? It had to be. Sending me a message. I underlined Gilligoole and Galway, then International Research Centre twice. I took my phone from my pocket, Googled 'International Research Centre, Galway', closed my eyes and prayed. I prayed that this crazy guess was right. That Mum's years of watching for a sign from other dragons had turned into her sign to me. I prayed that I'd find the phone number and listen to her perfectly reasonable explanation of what had happened. I prayed that in a few hours she'd be sitting right here on the sofa.

Nando once said that God always answers prayers. But not in the way you expect.

My dad said that too when I prayed my mum would come back. And he was right. God did answer. Not by returning my old mum, but by giving me a new one.

But now she'd gone too.

I sat at my desk. Tears dropped on to my English copy. After five minutes I gave up on homework and drew a picture instead — of the big fat bone I had to pick with God.

'Crap!' I shouted. 'Crappy damn crap! Crap dammy crappit!' The web page said:

International Research Centre (IRC)

The IRC is a centre for international government research based in County Galway, Ireland.

No map, no phone number. Nothing. I stared at it trying to squeeze out something useful. Government? But which bit of government? Come to think of it, which government? It said international. I looked at my notes again. *Local* firemen? Helpful as mud.

I went to Google Maps but nothing came up for International Research Centre. I looked up the Gilligoole Mountains. A strip of green along the Galway coast. This IRC place could be anywhere.

I called Charlotte and told her about the news report. Then – maybe it was the phone line, but I'd never heard her sound so gentle – 'Are you sure, Aidan?'

'About what?'

'Your mum starting the fire. It could have been caused by anything. I mean,' she cleared her throat, 'you've got to admit this is a pretty long shot.'

'Any shorter ones?' I snapped.

There was a long silence. At last she said, 'Has anything strange happened to your mum recently?'

'Apart from you finding out about her, and me starting school?' My voice rolled its eyes down the phone. 'Oh no-ho, nothing at all.'

She didn't deserve that. But she took it well. 'OK.' More silence. Then she said, 'I think I should tell my dad. Just that your mum's gone missing, not that she's a, you-know.'

'No way! He'll want to go straight to the gardaí. And when you say he can't, he'll start asking questions. And you may be smart in some ways, but I bet you're a rubbish liar.'

She didn't deny it, which I guess confirmed my theory. 'Let me tell him the truth, then. Maybe he'll think of something that doesn't involve the guards. Surely anything's better than this?'

Considering what the truth *was*, I wasn't sure at all. 'I need to sleep on it. We'll talk at school tomorrow.'

After a lifetime of keeping his mum's secret, he deserved one more night. 'OK. Sleep wel—' I clamped my stupid lips together. As if.

I HAVE TO TALK TO YOU

The sofa was surprisingly comfortable. I knew that because I spent most of the night lying awake on its surprising comfort. I kept the TV on for more news of the fire.

Nothing. The story had come and gone. I gave up and changed channels. A lady was chasing a man who fell into a swimming pool. I changed again to a dog riding a bicycle, except it wasn't really because a boy was holding its paws on the handlebars and its bum on the saddle. I switched off the telly. I switched off the light. I tried to switch off my brain.

Can you dream without sleeping? Because the next few hours were a string of wide-awake nightmares. Mum on the deck of a boat beckoning; as I waded into the water, the boat sped away. Mum climbing a mountain; as I watched from below, the rock crumbled and she fell off. Mum sinking in quicksand with a silent scream, stretching out a scaly hand that I couldn't reach.

I must have nodded off eventually because next time I looked at my phone it said 7.12. I ran upstairs and burst into Mum's bedroom, praying she'd be asleep in her bed and knowing that she wouldn't. I went into my bedroom, dressed for school and came downstairs. I felt like a robot, my movements automatic, my insides cold metal. I ate a piece of toast, not out of hunger but out of obedience to my operating instructions: *Ensure battery is charged before use.* I assembled my lunch with mechanical hands, put one foot in front of the other and walked to school left right left right.

I stopped in the yard. The chatter, the laughter, the running and shouting; my insides dissolved to goo. I forced myself in through the entrance, down the corridor and into class. I sat at my desk and put my head in my hands, listening to the scribble of voices as the room filled up.

'Aidan?'

It was barely a whisper. Maybe that's why I didn't recognise it. I'd never heard him whisper before. I looked up.

'I have to talk to you.' Phil's fringe hung over his eyes. 'In private.'

'Oh no you don't.' Charlotte had come up behind him. 'Whatever you say to Aidan you say to me too.'

I waited for his insult. But amazingly he just shrugged and turned towards the classroom door.

It's strange how a noisy corridor can be the most private place. Pupils pushed and chattered to their classes, ignoring us completely.

Phil tucked his fringe behind his ear. 'I know there's something weird going on.'

A plughole opened in my chest.

'Ever since I came to your house. Before then, my dad kept telling me to be nice to you. But after that Sunday, he said I should keep away.'

'Because our house isn't clean enough,' I said. 'Because you might catch something.'

'That's what he told me. But it's more than that.' Phil's face was tight and pale, as if it had shrunk in the wash. 'On the Wednesday after that, a man came to dinner. He had an American accent. He didn't give his name, just said he worked with Dad. I could tell he was a boss because Dad went all smarmy round him, and Mum made this really posh meal.'

I remembered my dinner at the Pardoes. 'Really posh' must be some feast.

'He was friendly, chatted about school. And then,' Phil blinked at me, 'he asked about you.'

'What?' My stomach squeezed tight.

'He said Dad had mentioned I had a friend who'd been homeschooled, and that I'd been to your house. He said he was thinking about homeschooling for his own kids. He asked about my visit – had your mam done any homeschooly stuff with us. I told him we'd cooked. It was weird how interested he was, specially after Dad had told me to keep away from you. I wanted to know why. So after dinner, when they went into Dad's study, I spied on them through the keyhole.'

He said it so matter-of-factly. Snooping was obviously no big deal for this steal-Mammy's-change, natural-born sneak.

The bell rang for class. Phil ignored it. 'Dad went to his desk and took an envelope out of a drawer. The man opened it and emptied something on to his palm. I couldn't see what because he cupped his fingers round it.' Phil was in a rush now, spilling out words like too-hot soup. 'But he seemed excited. Dad said, "Do you think it could be?" The man said he'd run some tests and get back to Dad as soon as he knew anything. Then he put whatever it was back in the envelope and –'

'*There* you are!' Miss Burkitt marched down the corridor. 'Didn't you hear the bell, Aidan? Charlotte?' She raised her eyebrows when she saw Phil. She'd noticed our rift over the last couple of weeks. 'Come on, you three. Class is starting.'

'Please,' I begged, 'just five more –'

'*Now.*' She shooed us towards the classroom.

No! Two whole hours until break. My stomach shrank. I hated Phil. I hated his dad. And just at that moment, I hated Miss Burkitt too.

SICK

We had maths first thing, or rather the rest of the class did. While they worked out the area of a swimming pool, I glared at the back of Phil's head. It was bent over his desk as he scribbled away. If only I could slice off the top like a boiled egg and scoop out everything he knew.

After a million years he raised his hand.

Miss Burkitt looked up from the front desk. 'Yes, Philip?'

'I don't feel well, Teacher.'

'What's wrong?'

'I'm all dizzy. Like I might throw up.'

'What, now?' Her eyes flew to the waste paper basket by the window. A snigger went round.

Phil blushed. 'Not *right* now. Can I go home?'

'No!' someone cried. As Miss Burkitt turned her head, I realised it was me.

Her eyebrows arched. 'Pardon?'

I swallowed. 'Sorry. But he can't.'

Now her eyebrows collided. 'What are you talking about, Aidan? Of course he can, if he's ill.'

'He's not,' Charlotte squeaked behind me. 'He's faking it.'

'Excuse me!' Miss Burkitt spread her palms on the desk. 'In case you hadn't noticed, *I'm* the teacher. And I don't want a bug going round.' Phil moaned in agreement, his head on the desk. 'Go to the office, Philip. Mrs Lynch will phone your mother.'

He made a big deal of staggering to his feet.

'You complete . . .' I muttered as he passed my desk, failing to find a word that meant gutless-spineless-chicken-turd.

Something fell on to my shoe. Phil headed out of the door. I leaned down and picked up a square of folded paper. I put it on my lap and opened it.

Philip Pardoe had *not* been sizing swimming pools.

Dear Aidan,

I'm writing this instead of telling it to your face in case you smash mine in. Please don't hate me.

I had a feeling I was going to. I bunched my fists on my lap.

When the American man left that night, I asked why he was so interested in you. Dad stuck to the homeschooling story but I could see he was lying. Over mid-term I kind of forgot about it, or at least gave up trying to figure it out. Then two nights ago, Dad's mobile rang at dinner. He has this rule that no one's allowed to answer calls when we're eating. But he took it and went out. I heard his voice go all smarmy, so I guessed it was the American boss calling. I told Mam I needed the bathroom. I went out and listened again at the study door. Dad was kind of gasping and saying things like 'Amazing' and 'Seriously?' Then he said something that really hit me. 'Tomorrow, when Aidan's at school.'

My heart jolted. Yesterday. Mum's disappearance.

Dad went to his desk and wrote something down. Then he repeated it down the phone – you know, to check he'd got it right. I had a pen in my pocket and wrote it on my hand. Dad ended the call. I was back at the table before Dad. After dinner I copied it on to paper and washed my hand so he wouldn't see. I have no idea what it means but maybe you do.

Boonkilly IRC 3431738.

The IRC! An electric shock went through me. Boonkilly – was that a place? And one, two . . . seven digits. A phone number?

I was going to tell you yesterday. But when you did that Troy thing, and everyone was buzzing round you, I guess I was jealous.

I banged my fists together, wishing Phil's head was between them. If I'd known all this yesterday, maybe I could have stopped Mum's kidnap. I had no idea how, but at least it gave me more reason to hate Phil.

Dad didn't come home last night. Mam said he's away for a few days for work. I got a bad feeling and I couldn't sleep. I haven't a clue what's going on. But I bet you have. And now I've told you, maybe you'll for-give me.

I snorted so loudly that everyone as far as Andy Dunne, four desks away, turned their heads. As soon as the bell rang for break I ran out of the classroom and down the corridor towards the secretary's office.

I saw you go. And I wasn't far behind.

Thank goodness Phil was still there. And thank goodness the secretary had popped out. He was sitting in the corner with his head bowed, doing the sick act.

I bent over his chair and squeezed his upper arms till I felt bone. 'What else do you know?' I whisper-roared.

He looked up. 'Nothing.' His face was lumpy and yellowish like a potato. 'I've told you everything.'

Charlotte stood beside me. She looked up from Phil's letter, which I'd shoved into her hand.

'Why are you suddenly helping us, when you've worked really really hard not to before?'

'I was just doing what I was told then. My dad – he kind of scares me sometimes. And he's scaring me now.' Phil blinked miserably. 'I don't know what he's doing, but I know it involves you. And I'm pretty sure it isn't good. The thing is –' his mouth twisted, as if what he had to say was really hard work, 'I like your mam. She's fun, and so easy-going. Mine just tells me off all the time.'

Poor ickle Phil. I squeezed even harder. 'Does she know anything?'

'I don't think so. She's –'

'Shhh!' Charlotte hissed.

Because there she was, standing in the doorway. I dropped my arms and stepped back.

'Philip,' she said, 'what's wrong? I got a call at the hairdresser's.' She looked annoyed. 'You were fine this morning.'

'He nearly threw up in class,' Charlotte said. Mrs Pardoe glared at her. But she was no match for the Queen of Scowl. 'You've got to take him home.'

I couldn't believe it! Charlotte was helping Phil.

He needed it. From the look on your face, if he didn't leave then, he wouldn't survive the day. Plus, I sort of admired what he'd done. It took guts to go against his dad, and to admit he was jealous. That couldn't have been easy for him.

What about me? Thanks to him my mother was missing!

It's over now. Give him a break.

After what happened? Give *me* a break.

THE ISLAND OF ITALY

Phil's mum hustled him out. Charlotte and I reread the letter as the bell rang for the end of break.

'I'll get my phone,' I said. 'I'm going to call that number.'

Charlotte followed me into the corridor. 'Hang on,' she said. 'If it *is* that IRC place, what will you say? "Hi, this is Aidan Mooney. Sorry to bother you, but I think you've kidnapped my mother."'

I stopped. 'So what do you suggest?'

She bit her thumbnail. 'We need to think this through. Maybe start by looking up Boonkilly.'

Back in the classroom, I took out my phone and went to Google Maps. We'd just found Boonkilly, a tiny dot north of Galway City, when Miss Burkitt came in. I shoved the phone under my desk.

During geography, she gave out a map of Italy. While the others filled in the cities, I wrote out possible phone conversations.

1. Me: Is that the IRC? May I speak to Mrs Shauna Mooney?

    IRC: She's actually busy right now, being held hostage.

2. Me: This is Sergeant/Detective/Superintendent Mooney/Meaney/Heaney. I believe you've kidnapped a Mrs S. Mooney.

    IRC: Sorry, wrong number.

3. Me: Give my mum back NOW.

    IRC: Sure, when you give us €1000,000,000,000,000.

'Aidan?'

I looked up.

'I said, what's the name of the island at the bottom of Italy?' Miss Burkitt was holding up the handout. She jabbed it with a pen.

'Um.' I blinked. 'The island of . . . Italy?'

She clicked her tongue. 'For goodness sake. It's Sicily. What's wrong with you today?'

It was raining at lunchtime so everyone had to stay in the classroom to eat their sandwiches. Charlotte came over to my desk. She opened her lunchbox. 'I did some baking last night,' she said almost shyly. 'To cheer you up.'

'Thanks.' I forced a smile. But when I smelt sharp, sweet ginger, and saw the pile of Cyclopses, each with one raisin eye, I thought of Troy-on-a-tray and Mum. 'Actually, I'm not very hungry.'

I nodded and felt like a dork. 'Sorry. Gingerbread's the only thing I can do.'

Andy Dunne came over. 'More story food?'

'Brilliant,' said Kennedy behind him.

Aidan was having trouble holding his face together.

'Yeah,' I said. 'Come over to my desk and I'll tell you about Odysseus blinding the Cyclops.

By the end of lunch break, half the class had eaten a gingerbread Polyphemus and heard how Odysseus and his men escaped from the Cyclops's cave by clinging upside down to the bellies of sheep. Then they wanted another story, so I told them how the witch Circe turned everyone except Odysseus into pigs. And then how the Lotus eaters made them forget home so that Odysseus had to drag them back and chain them to their ship till they got over it. Even Dan, Ben and Tom hung round the edges, keen to listen now that Phil was out of the way. Everyone loved it. I would've done too if it hadn't stopped me talking to Aidan. I saw him sitting with his head bent over his desk. He was probably on his phone, or at least pretending to be, so that no one would disturb him.

It wasn't till the end of school that we had some privacy. 'Your mum's been gone a whole day,' I said as we walked across the yard. 'We've got to tell my dad. Come home with me. You can't spend the weekend alone in your house.'

'I won't,' I said, going through the school gate. 'I'll be on a train.'

'What?!' Charlotte squeached (squeak-screeched) so loudly that two fourth-classers crossing the road looked round. 'Your mum's been kidnapped, Aidan. It's far too dangerous.'

'You think I don't know that? But I can't just sit at home waiting for a call.'

'I told you, come and stay with me.'

I shook my head. 'I've got a lead to follow now.

And anyway, I couldn't act like everything's normal in front of your dad.'

'I guess not. Well, let *me* come with *you*, then.'

Now it was me who squeached. 'No way! What if something happened to you?'

She put her hands on her hips. 'Well hello – same for you.'

'It's not. Your dad would never forgive me. And anyway, what would you tell him? That we're off on a weekend break to Galway?'

For once she was stuck for an answer. While she did fish impersonations, I said, 'Look, it's *my* mother. You need to stay with your dad and mind your own business.'

The look she gave me could out-gorgon the Gorgon. 'I can't. Believe. You said that.' Then she turned round and stomped off.

I couldn't believe it either. But at least it stopped her arguing. How could I put her in danger when everything was my fault? I walked home, iffing miserably. If I hadn't befriended Phil . . . if I hadn't forced Mum to let him come over . . . if we'd never met the Pardoes . . . if I hadn't begged to go to school in the first place, none of this would have happened.

Whatever 'this' was.

I stopped at our front gate and touched the burn mark on the post. Who had terrified Mum out of her newly found breath control? I went down the drive and unlocked the door, my heart in my toes. The hall was so silent, the kitchen so sad: just as I'd left it, with my breakfast plate on the table and bits of ham on the counter. No smiling Mum to pour me a drink and ask about my day.

I sat at the table and unfolded Phil's letter. I had to try that number. The voice, or voicemail, at the other end might give a clue, and I could end the call without speaking.

I Googled the code for Galway and rang.

But all I got was a man's voice saying, 'The number you have dialled is not available.'

I pressed END CALL like a torturer poking out a victim's eye. I put the phone on my lap and my hands on the table, and sat for what felt like a week. Then I put the phone on the table and my hands in my lap, and sat for what felt like two more.

The doorbell rang. I jumped up, ran down the hall and opened the door.

'Oh.' I swallowed. 'I thought it might be . . . hi.'

'Hi.' Charlotte had a rucksack slung over her shoulder. She turned and waved her dad's taxi off. 'He says thank you, by the way.'

I blinked. 'What for?'

'Inviting me over. He's on the late shift, so he's really glad I won't be on my own. He said it's super-nice of you to let me stay for a sleepover, *and* all day tomorrow, and actually till Sunday, because he's on lates all weekend.'

'But –'

'But like you said, I'm a rubbish liar,' she went on. 'So you need to invite me right now. Then I'll be like the Greek Oracle who told the truth, only *before* it happened.' She came into the hall and dumped her rucksack on the bottom stair.

'I don't understand,' I said.

'It's very simple,' she said quietly. I don't mean shy quietly or scared quietly. I mean completely-determined-my-mind's-made-up-this-is-final quietly. 'I'm coming with you.'

'But I told you to mind your own –'

'This *is* my business. You're my friend. And your mum is too. And you'll need someone to help find her. And I'm good at working things out. And if anything goes wrong I'll be your back-up. And I've nicked two packets of custard creams for the train. And if you don't let me come I'll tell my dad everything, because your plan is crazy-stupid.'

I held up my hands. 'OK, OK. I realised by "custard creams" that I'm not going to stop you.'

She nodded. 'That's the most sensible thing you've said all day.' She pointed to her rucksack. 'Hat, gloves, phone, charger, extra jumper, above-mentioned custard creams, and *Legendary Journeys of Ancient Greece*. What have you packed?'

'Definitely not a book. Do you seriously think you'll be reading?'

She gave me a look that could shrivel a turnip. 'Do you seriously *think*?'

For the first time since yesterday, I smiled. A light was rising inside me, tiny and bright, like the lamp of an angler fish, deep in the ocean. It wasn't exactly hope but a kind of relief that I wasn't alone, and that we – what a teeny, brilliant word – were doing something, not waiting for something to be done. Even the dead-end phone number didn't seem such a problem now that Charlotte was here.

'Maybe Phil wrote it down wrongly,' she said when I told her. 'And now we're going there anyway, so we don't really need it. What's for dinner?'

In the kitchen I heated up some bits and pieces in a saucepan while Charlotte went on her phone and costed the journey I'd worked out at lunchtime. 'I got money off Dad to buy pizzas,' she said. 'I told him it would be a nice thank you for all the cooking you've done for me.'

I turned from the stove. 'Good one.'

'It's enough for two child returns to Galway,' she said. 'But there's the bus fare to Boonkilly, and we'll need food too.'

'We can pack sandwiches. And –' I turned back to the saucepan so she wouldn't see my face. For a second I felt like thieving Phil. But only a second.

It was hardly stealing if it brought Mum back. 'There'll be a purse in Mum's bag. It's in the sitting room.'

I had to admit that his crazy-stupid plan was coming together. And also that it was the best sausage-egg-tomato-mustard-yoghurt-cornflakes risotto I'd ever tasted.

EIGHT O'CLOCK ON SATURDAY MORNING

'Who are you texting?' I said, as we finished off the SETMYC risotto for breakfast.

'Dad. Just to say that your home number isn't working so if he needs me, call my mobile.'

'Wow.' I raised my eyebrows. 'An actual lie.'

'Is not. If he phones this house, no one will answer, which is the same as not working.'

I knew better than to argue. We made a pile of cheese sandwiches and divided them between our rucksacks. 'In case we get separated,' I said. That led on to all sorts of unhelpful thoughts, which I tried to push out by tidying the kitchen for Mum's return.

We left the house, went down the road, turned left at the Spar then right into the high street. At the far end was Drumadea train station, an echoey building where people rushed and gabbled into phones, full of hurry and importance even on a Saturday.

The excitement that had danced in my chest overnight sank to a wriggling dread. We were alone. No one knew where we were going. I glanced at Charlotte, marching beside me, her curls stuffed inside a stupid green bobbly thing.

It's called a hat, Aidan. I knew it would be freezing on the west coast.

What if something went wrong? Her dad would never forgive me – if there was a me to forgive. I should never have let her come. But sure, I was glad that I had.

We bought our tickets and waited on the platform for the 9.40 to Galway. Charlotte found a vending machine and came back with two cans of Coke. Nice idea, but just looking at them made me feel sick.

The train roared into the station. We found window seats.

Your face was like nougat: white with nutty freckles. I let you sit facing forwards. Puking was *not* an option.

NUMBER JUMBLE

I stared through the window as the west rushed towards us. Stone walls wandered across fields. Sheep sprinkled the hillsides like woolly grains of rice. In the distance, a glittering mist merged the sky and land. I tried to imagine where Mum might be, what she might be doing.

Bad idea. I tried to unimagine.

'Earth calling Mooneyland.' Charlotte tapped the table between us. I turned to face her.

'That number,' she said, 'in Phil's letter. Maybe he didn't get it wrong. If everything's so secret, maybe his dad wrote it down in code, in case someone found it.'

'I thought you said we didn't need to ring now we're going to the IRC anyway.'

She shrugged. 'Fine. Just thought you might be interested.'

I knew she was dying to show me her code-cracking skills. I pulled out the letter from my trouser pocket and slid it across the table. 'Go on then, brainbox.'

She unfolded the sheet. 'It would have to be hidden from other people, but not so hidden that he'd forget it himself. The easiest thing would be to write it backwards.' She looked down the page for the number Phil had written. 'That would be 8371343.'

I took my phone from my anorak pocket and rang. 'The number you have dialled is not available,' said the same man's voice as yesterday.

Charlotte frowned at the letter. 'How about every other number – first, third and fifth – then the ones in between, second and fourth?'

We tried that. Forwards – 3378413, and backwards – 8733314.

We tried all the even numbers forwards then backwards. We tried all the odd numbers forwards and backwards.

I made a paper aeroplane and threw it at your nose.

CASSANDRA'S PUPPY

We arrived in Galway just after midday. The sky was a nervous grey, as if it knew rain was coming and didn't want to break the bad news.

'Where now?' Charlotte said.

I took the timetable I'd printed out of my anorak pocket. 'There's a bus to Boonkilly in just over an hour.' It left from the station, so we sat in the café, ordered two hot chocolates and sneak-ate a packet of custard creams from Charlotte's rucksack.

I hate stations. I think of them as leaving places, where you go to run away. That's silly, I know, because they're arriving places too. But everything's so sad: the cold grey walls, the tired grey travellers and the wet grey ground that looks as if it's been crying.

They do good hot chocolate, though. We wrapped our hands round the paper cups and sipped hot, sweet comfort.

'What do we do when we get to Boonkilly?' Charlotte said.

I took the lid off my cup. 'Look around,' I said vaguely, realising that I hadn't planned anything beyond arriving there. I bent my head, warming my nose in hot chocolate steam. I swear I could *feel* her eyes rolling.

We got on the bus at 1.30. It took us out of Galway, through soft, curving hills like fuzzy-felt. The sea appeared, a silver line in the distance. We drove through villages and fields with slow-eyed cows. After an hour and a bit we arrived in Boonkilly.

It's a tiny village, not much more than a street with brightly painted houses and a pub. *A good thing and a bad thing*, I thought as we got off the bus. Good because it shouldn't be hard to find the IRC with so few other buildings. Bad because it would be hard for us to sniff around unnoticed.

It was freezing, with a mean little wind that pinched my face and ears. I put on gloves and pulled up the hood of my anorak, wishing I'd brought my own stupid bobbly thing – sorry, hat.

Charlotte pointed down the street. At the end of the village there was a building with a petrol pump outside and a sign above: Geraghty's Store 'n' More. 'Let's ask in there,' she said. 'It's beyond the other houses. Less chance of attracting attention.'

Not that there was any to attract. The village street was deserted. Even at the shop we had to ring the bell three times before a lady unlocked the door. She opened it with one hand and put the other to her mouth to cover a yawn.

'Sorry, dears.' She had a flat, round face like a friendly plate. 'Caught me napping.' She patted her white candy floss hair, as if that too needed waking up. 'Come in.'

She swept her arm back to welcome us into the shop. I got the feeling that business didn't exactly boom in Boonkilly.

'It's OK,' I said awkwardly. 'Can you tell us where the IRC is?'

She frowned. 'That government place?' She pointed over my left shoulder. 'See that hill? It's in the woods at the top. There was a fire there the other day.'

Charlotte glanced at me. 'How do you get there?' she said.

'There's a road up the hill.' The lady narrowed her eyes. 'Why? You can't go there. It's private property.'

'But –' Charlotte's hand went to her mouth. Then – of all the things to say when you're trying not to attract attention – 'Our mum said it was a dog rescue centre.'

The lady snorted.

'We were going to get a puppy.' Charlotte's voice wobbled.

'Oh.' The lady swallowed her laugh. 'I'm sorry, dear. You won't find one there.'

'Thanks anyway,' I said, grabbing Charlotte's hand. 'Come on, Cassandra. Mum's waiting.'

We ran off down the street.

Cassandra? What's that you said about not attracting attention?

We turned left off the main street down a little road towards the hill. The sky dropped threads of rain, like a woolly grey jumper unravelling. We passed a row of cottages, a farmhouse and a barn full of hay. The tarmac gave way to a dirt track. It took us up the hill and into the woods. We stopped and ate a couple of damp sandwiches from our rucksacks, though my stomach was gurgling from nerves rather than hunger.

Raindrops tutted on the leaves around us, as if disapproving of our stupid plan. My nose stung with cold. The track steepened. Daylight was fading, though my watch only said 4.15. None of this was encouraging. But it was a beach in Barbados compared to the clearing we reached half an hour later.

It was hard to tell through the trees, but I guessed we were near the top of the hill. The path ended at a steel fence more than twice my height.

It was flanked either side by trees. Behind the fence stood a low, rectangular building. It had a front door but no windows. Between the building and the fence was a yard where three cars were parked. There was a gate in the fence, bolted and padlocked, with a metal box in the side: probably an intercom. In front of the fence, on the path, stood a notice.

INTERNATIONAL RESEARCH CENTRE

GOVERNMENT PROPERTY

STRICTLY NO ADMITTANCE

TRESPASSERS WILL BE PROSECUTED

The trees either side of the sign were black skeletons. My heart dropped a mile. 'Mum,' I murmured, picturing her screaming, flaming arrival in this desolate place.

I put a finger to my lips and dragged you off the path.

TROY STORY 2

'Now what?' We'd been crouching in the trees for hours – OK, fourteen minutes – watching the building. An oily darkness was sliding into the sky. The rain fell steadily, tapping branches and twitching leaves. The ground was a tangle of roots and fallen twigs. I put my rucksack against a tree, sat on a root and leaned back. My bum froze. The woods smelled like wet socks – or maybe it was just my wet socks.

I'd imagined an 'International Research Centre' would be a busy place, with people coming and going, where we could slip unnoticed through the open gate. But this? Not a person in sight, a gate with a padlock as big as my fist and a fence we could never climb.

A crow creaked off a branch and spread in the sky like a flapping moustache. Cold pressed into my bones. Whatever watery hope I'd had was disappearing down the plughole.

I nudged Charlotte. 'Hey, I said now what?'

'I heard you,' she muttered. She'd been staring at the gate for ages. Now she turned to me. 'We press the intercom.'

'What? You think they're going to let in two kids who've come snooping through the woods? Don't be an idiot!'

As in 'idios', an Ancient Greek word.

As in Ancient Greeks.

As in Ancient Greek legends.

One legend in particular.

The legend of a city. A city with a wall. A wall they couldn't get through. Until they made a present and they left it at the gate.

There are some words that have to be said, even though they'd rather stay sitting on your tongue. When Charlotte explained her idea, I forced them out. 'You're amazing.'

She bowed her head. 'With a little help from Odysseus.'

We crept round the darkening woods, gathering branches and pine cones. My stomach did cartwheels as I loaded them into her arms. 'Are you sure about this?'

She made a face that could freeze Florida. 'You mean are *you* sure?'

She hugged the bundle to her chest. Then she crouch-ran across the path and along the front of the fence. At the far end she dropped the bundle.

She knelt down and made a pile of the branches and cones. She took off her gloves and stuck each one on a branch. And there it was: our version of the wooden horse of Troy. From where I sat, peering through the gloom, it looked more like a wooden reindeer, hopefully weird enough to warrant closer inspection.

Charlotte ran back to the gate. She hesitated for a second, then pressed the intercom. Five seconds later she was by my side again. I swear I could hear her heart beating. She pointed to the building. I pressed my hand to my mouth. The front door was opening. A sensor light went on above it. The powerful beam crashed through the dusk, lighting up the whole courtyard.

A woman came out. She was short and stocky. She shut the door, crossed the yard to the gate and looked round. She held a torch in one hand and a key in the other. She undid the padlock, slid back the bolt and opened the gate. As she shone the torch our way I got a better look. Her hair was wrenched into a bun. She had a face like a Marmite-hater who's just eaten Marmite.

A twig snapped under my foot. The woman shielded her eyes with a hand and took a step in our direction. I shrank against the tree trunk. Then – oh thank you – she turned and shone the torch the other way. Seeing Charlotte's bundle, she gave a squeak. She strode towards it.

'Now!' Charlotte hissed. I felt a shove in my back. It launched me across the path and through the open gate. I shot across the yard and dived behind a car just as the light above the front door went off. I looked across the dusky courtyard. On the other side of the fence, the woman had her back to me. She was standing by the pile of cones, shining her torch along the path I'd come from.

'We made it!' I whispered.

We. That teeny word again. But this time not so brilliant. Because when I looked over my shoulder, Charlotte wasn't there.

I lay at the edge of the path. For a second my ankle felt numb. Then pain rushed in. In the fading light I saw the woman spin round and shine the torch my way. She must have heard me trip on the root and thud to the ground. She walked back along the fence towards me.

I tried not to blink. I tried not to breathe. Thank goodness for my dark brown anorak and green bobble hat — not so stupid now, hey — that I prayed would disguise me as a fallen branch.

My heart was thumping like a fist on a door. I shrank against the side of the car. I could just make out the woman's shape at the gate. She turned once more towards the path where I'd last seen Charlotte. I took deep breaths. Panic wasn't an option right now.

The woman paused. Then, using her torch, she came in through the gate, closed it, slid the bolt across and snapped the padlock shut. Her heels clicked towards me across the courtyard. I shrank lower to escape the torch beam. *Please walk past me.* Click click. *Please walk past me.* Click click. *Please walk . . .* CLICK CLICK . . . *Yes!* She'd reached the front door. The sensor light went on again.

This was the hard bit, where she and the door had to help me. *Don't turn round*, I begged the woman, and *shut slowly*, I commanded the door. She punched a code into a keypad above the handle. I squatted on my toes, ready to sneak in behind her.

Still lying by the path, I saw the woman open the front door. She stepped inside. Turning round, she gave one last look in my direction. Then she slammed the door. Oh no. Oh no no. Aidan was locked out . . . and in.

MY TURN TO BE AMAZING

I sat on the concrete and hugged my knees. I couldn't go back: the gate was padlocked, the fence too high to climb. I couldn't go forward: although I'd been watching the woman carefully, I wasn't close enough to see the code.

The code. Something flickered at the edge of my brain. I hadn't seen the numbers . . . but I'd seen the number of *times* she'd pressed the keypad at the door. Somehow that felt important. As the sensor light went off again, it hit me.

The door?

Duh, the number. Seven. That's how many digits there were in Phil's code. We'd ruled it out as a phone number. Could it be the door code? It was worth a try. Excitement fizzed through me like a tablet in water. Before it could dissolve, I got to my feet and crept towards the door.

There was a quack. I stumbled backwards. What was a duck doing in my pocket? Oh yes. My ringtone. I took out my phone. 'Where are you?' I whispered.

'Off the path,' came Charlotte's voice, 'back where we were before you ran. I fell over a root. The woman heard me, so I had to lie there till she went in. How do we get you out?'

'We don't. We get me in.' I told her my hunch about the code. Taking Phil's letter out of my pocket, I reached the door. The light came on above, illuminating the keypad. 'Oh,' I said faintly. 'No.'

'What?'

'It's not numbers. It's letters.'

There was a long silence. Beyond the courtyard fence, all was darkness. It was filling my insides too. 'You still there?' I tried not to sound as if I was holding back tears.

'I'm thinking,' she said. More silence. Then 'Hey! The Ancient Greeks didn't use digits.'

'So?'

'They used the Greek alphabet to represent numbers. Maybe Mr Pardoe turned the letters into numbers. The simplest thing would be 1 for A, 2 for B and so on.'

'OK.' I held the phone light over Phil's letter. 'The first number's 3. So that would be C.'

'Try it.'

I hunched my shoulder to keep the phone against my ear. I held Phil's letter in front of me

144

and converted the numbers. '3 is C.' I jabbed the keypad. '4 is D.' My gloved finger was clumsy with nerves. '3 again, that's C. 1 is A, 7 is . . .' I counted in my head, 'G. Then 3 for C again. And 8 is . . . H.' My heart was playing pinball. 'Here goes.' I turned the handle.

'Well?' Charlotte said.

I scooped out my voice from my throat. 'Still locked.' Phil's letter fell from my shaking hand. 'Now what do I –?'

There was a whooshy noise down the phone, like waves on a pebbly beach. I stood up. Pain shot through my ankle. I bit my top lip. 'Aidan?' I limped on to the path. 'Are you OK?' Standing on the track, I could see him in the light of the sensor above the door.

Down the phone I heard his quick breathing. Then he said the strangest thing. 'Believe.'

'What?'

'I just dropped Phil's letter,' he said. 'I picked it up the wrong way. If you screw up your eyes and look at the numbers upside down, they kind of look like a word.'

Without the darkness I'd never have seen it. In daylight they'd just look like upturned numbers. But with a bit of squinting, a lot of imagination and all that talk of numbers being letters, I could almost BELIEVE it spelled just that. And if you don't BELIEVE me, try scrunching up your eyes and imagining that you're cold, wet, scared and desperate to get through a door that will lead you to your mum who's been taken by some weird government people who you're terrified have discovered her deepest secret.

Before Charlotte could pooh-pooh the idea, I pressed B on the keypad. Then E, then L, I, E then V, then . . .

'I don't believe it,' I breathed. 'I mean, I *do* believe it. I mean, can you believe it?!'

'What?'

'I'm in!'

'Oh my gosh,' she said. 'Oh my gosh. Oh my –'

The next word was kind of obvious, so I knew she'd forgive me for interrupting.

'Wait there,' I said. 'Don't phone me inside, it'll make too much noise. I'll text you when I find anything.'

Charlotte's voice was panicky. 'But what if they find you first and –?'

I pressed END CALL. There were so many ways to finish that sentence and none of them was helpful. I wrapped them all in mental loo roll and flushed them down my mind toilet, along with other stinking possibilities, like *I'm mad* and *This is beyond stupid*. I put my phone and my brain on silent. I slipped the phone and Phil's letter into my pocket. Then I pushed the door softly. I don't know why I bothered with the softly. My heart was a drum that could wake the dead.

But it seemed there were no dead people to

wake, or even living ones. Just a long, brightly lit corridor that ended in double doors. It was super-clean, with white walls and shiny white floor tiles. I blinked in the glare and took off my muddy trainers. Hugging them to my chest, I snuck down the corridor in my socks.

My phone buzzed. I took it from my pocket.

Anything?

I texted back:

Gimme a chance

I came to a door on the left. There was a window at eye level. The sensible thing would be to duck as I passed. But sensible things hadn't got me here. Peeking through, I saw a room, bright and white-walled like the corridor. It was bare except for a bed along the left-hand wall. A woman sat on top. Her head was bent over a book. She wore jeans, a blue T-shirt and the strangest headgear. It was a white cone, like one of those medieval princess hats only shorter.

I crept on. Further down the corridor was another door with a window. I looked through to a second room, just like the first except the bed was on the right. A man lay facing the wall. He wore a shirt like an old-fashioned peasant smock, baggy and white with – I caught my breath – red blotches near the top. Was he asleep or –? He stirred slightly, thank goodness. I breathed again.

There was a third door on the left. I looked

through the window. And never mind the sneaking, forget the need for silence . . . I squeached. In half a heartbeat I'd turned the handle – not locked! – and shot across the room. I dropped my shoes and threw myself at the bed, hugging and kissing and blasting the ears off the woman sitting on top, who looked ready to pop with amazement. 'MUUUM!'

I sat against the tree and shone my phone torch on the building. It loomed like a headache, even blacker than the surrounding air. I checked my messages. Nothing more.

I turned off the torch. Monsters grew from the gloom: skeleton trees pointing bony fingers; rain like ghostly footsteps on the leaves; cold, wet worms wriggling through my sleeves. I hugged myself and racked my brain for stories of rescue plans. Hercules tricking the giant Atlas into taking the world back on to his shoulders. Perseus holding up a mirrored shield to turn Medusa to stone. Theseus unravelling a ball of wool to guide him back out of the labyrinth. All of them outwitted their enemies. But all of them *knew* their enemies. There was no Greek legend about a boy going into a building and failing to text.

KIDDO

Mum's arms around me, her smell of honey on toast: I wanted to stay there forever. 'Are you OK?' I mumbled into her shoulder. 'What have they done to you? I saw a man sleeping. There was blood on his shirt.'

'Aidan.' She kissed my cheek. 'I'm fine. And the man is too.' She smoothed my hair with her claws.

Her claws. My stomach sank. She wasn't wearing gloves. Of course I'd guessed already that her secret was out. But guessing is different from seeing.

'Who kidnapped you, Mum? What is this place?'

She pushed me back gently and held my shoulders. 'How on earth did you find me? Her face was pale in the cold white light. 'I thought they weren't letting anyone in.'

'Aren't you glad to see me?' I pulled away.

'Course I am.' She hugged me again. 'It's just – how did you get here?'

I took off my gloves and stuffed them in my anorak pocket. 'How did *you* get here? And if you're OK, why didn't you tell me? How could you just –'

There was a squawk. Something gripped the top of my head. Or rather some things, like nails, dug into my scalp. I yelled. My hands flew to my head. With another squawk the nails let go. There was a rush of air, a flash of red. A bird landed on the headboard of Mum's bed.

At first glance it wasn't like any bird I'd seen. At second glance it was like two that I had, mixed into a firework of a creature. It had a parrot-shaped body and beak. Its long tail and colours were like a golden pheasant's with a thousand volts shot through: glittering oranges, reds and yellows.

There was a rap of footsteps. I spun round. A man strode through the open door. The bird took off again and landed on his head, screeching.

'What the . . . ?' The man threw out his arms in a kind of furious amazement.

'Please.' Mum put her arm round my shoulder. 'It's OK. This is my son, Aidan.'

'And this,' the man snapped, 'is private property. He was tall and thin and wore a white lab coat. 'How the hell did you get in?'

I swallowed.

'It was me.' Mum squeezed my shoulder. 'The intercom buzzed. Dana must have been busy; she didn't answer. When I heard his voice, I had to let him in. He came all the way from Drumadea to find me, Doctor. He's only twelve. I'm sure you can understand how worried he was.'

I wasn't sure at all from the look in his light blue eyes. An army of expressions marched through them: anger, alarm, uncertainty. Then he seemed to decide something. His face softened and he said in a calmer voice, 'I guess so.' His voice had settled to a smooth American drawl.

American? I gasped. 'Are you the man who visited the Pardoes?'

He ignored the question. 'How in sweet Hershey did you figure out . . . ?' He frowned, then nodded with a kind of grudging admiration. 'Smart kid.' The bird flew off his head and clatter-landed on the headboard again. 'So whaddya think?'

'I told you, Aidan,' Mum said quickly, 'I'm fine.'

'There ya go.' The doctor smiled. He had perfect teeth. With his tanned face and sandy hair, he looked as if he was made of vitamins and sunshine and tennis. 'She said it herself. So you can go now, kiddo. I'll have my man drive you to a hotel. He'll sort out a train ticket for tomorrow. Mom'll be home Monday evening.'

Perhaps it was the relief of finding her, perhaps fear at the thought of leaving her again, or anger at his condescending tone: something brought tears to the back of my eyes. 'Please let me stay.' I blinked madly. 'It's only one more day.'

'Sorry, kiddo. No can do.'

That was the final patronising straw. I turned on Mum. 'I didn't know where you were!' The bird on the headboard flapped its wings. 'For all I knew you could've been . . . how could you do that to me?'

Mum's shoulders sagged. 'I didn't,' she said quietly. 'And I'm so sorry, darling. I can imagine how awful it must have been.' She reached out to hug me but I pushed her away.

'No you can't! If you could, you'd let me stay now.'

She sat on the bed. 'I'd love to. But that's not my call.'

The doctor folded his arms. There was kindness in his eyes now, and sympathy.

'If you knew what this was about,' he said to me, 'you'd see why we have to keep it top secret.'

'And you think I won't?' I cried. 'I'm the best secret-keeper in the world. Aren't I, Mum?' A blast of rage hit me so hard that my legs felt weak. I had to sit down next to her, though I didn't want to. She was the one I was furious with. What secret could be bigger than the one I'd kept for her all my life? And this was my thanks!

Maybe some of my anger flowed into her, or maybe she felt bad about what I'd been through. Either way, she cleared her throat and said, 'Aidan's right, Doctor. You can trust him completely. Please let him stay.'

The man's eyes went hard again. Before he could speak I blurted out, 'I saw a man asleep. With bloodstains. If you send me home, I'll tell the guards. And the newspapers and the TV. They'll get reporters here and –'

'OK, OK.' He held up his hand like a policeman stopping traffic. 'I hear ya.' The muscles round his eyes went tight. 'Mom has a point. I guess I can trust you.'

Yes! My heart did a victory punch. But I pressed my lips together. It was too soon to smile. And I wished he'd stop 'Mom'-ing me.

He ran a hand over his hair. 'But it sure complicates things. You're gonna have to promise not to tell a soul what we're doing here. At least, not for a few months until we're ready. Then the whole world can know. And believe me, it'll be worth the wait. But in the meantime, mom's the word, eh?' He winked in a jokey way that somehow wasn't jokey at all. 'Does anyone else know you're here?'

Charlotte! In the thrill of finding Mum, I'd forgotten to text her. I might have won his trust but, until he'd won mine, no way would I tell him that she was outside, ready to go for help. 'No.'

My hand must have twitched towards my anorak pocket because suddenly he was by my side, whisking out my phone. 'Good. Let's keep it that way.' He moved as smoothly as liquid: not water but something strong and shiny like golden syrup.

'But I –'

'Won't need it while you're here.' There was steel in his smile. Was he daring me to make a fuss and rouse his suspicion that I wanted to contact someone?

He turned off my phone and slipped it into the breast pocket of his lab coat. 'Now, kiddo, I need you to sign something. You heard of the Official Secrets Act?'

'Sort of.' I shifted my bum on the bed and tried not to stare at his pocket.

'It's a law that protects government information. If you break it, that's a serious crime against the state.'

I looked at Mum. 'Have you signed it?'

She nodded. 'We all have.'

'Who's we?'

The doctor shook his head. 'Not until you've signed. Capeesh?'

I nodded in what I hoped was a capeeshy way, though there wasn't one single thing I understood about this strange, scary man and his strange, scary bird as they glided and squawked out of the door.

I unlocked my phone for the millionth time. Two minutes since I'd last looked, and eighteen since Aidan had texted. I jabbed the keys.

What's happening? ANSWER ME.

I counted to twenty. I started again. At fifty-three I closed my eyes. 'Come ON,' I said, 'you —' then two words Dad had taught me once, when he hammered his thumb instead of the IKEA bookshelf he was putting up.

Dad. He'd be starting his shift now, happy that I was having fun at Aidan's house. I opened my eyes and pressed my phone again.

Hi Dad, hope you had a good day. We're toasting marshmallows.

I'd read somewhere that details make lies more believable.

I just dropped one in the fire. It looks like a melted earthworm. See you tomorrow eve. C X☺X

SECRETS

'Who is that man?' I said as his footsteps faded down the corridor.

Mum put her hand on my knee. 'Wait until you sign. Why don't you tell me how you found me?'

I'd hardly got past the TV report on the fire when the doctor reappeared. He came over to the bed and handed me a pen and a sheet of paper.

IRISH STATUTE BOOK   OFFICE OF THE
ATTORNEY GENERAL

OFFICIAL SECRETS ACT 1963
AN ACT TO PROVIDE FOR THE
SAFEGUARDING OF OFFICIAL INFORMATION

Under the Official Secrets Act 1963 I, _____, agree not to communicate any information I learn at the International Research Centre to any other person or organisation until officially permitted to do so. If break this agreement, I will be guilty of an offence under the Official Secrets Act and will be arrested and tried in a court of law. On conviction I shall be liable to imprisonment for a term between two and seven years.*

I hereby agree to the above terms.

Signed _____ Date _____

*or an equivalent punishment for a minor

I signed it before I could worry what the 'equivalent punishment for a minor' might be.

'Good job.' The doctor folded the paper, put it in his pocket and flashed his brilliant smile. 'Now we can really say hi.' He held out his hand. 'Pleased to meet you, Aidan Mooney. Doctor Leviticus Krinsky the Third.' His grip was strong, his fingers long with nail tips like crescent moons. 'Thanks for lending us Mom for a couple days.'

'Lending?'

Now that I'd signed, he seemed to relax. His eyes were summer skies. He patted my shoulder. 'She's agreed to help us out.'

I pulled my hand away and stood up from the bed. 'You kidnapped her!'

He pretend-winced. 'Strong word, kiddo. Let's say I arranged her visit.' He looked at his watch. 'Gotta get on. Mom can fill you in.' He turned to the door. 'Dana!'

Quick footsteps approached down the corridor. A figure appeared in the doorway. I recognised the chunky woman who'd come to the gate. She had tiny black eyes and a mouth like a staple. She glared at me. 'Who on earth is this?' Her voice was as sharp as a bag of toenails. 'And who let him in?' She looked so cross that I almost said, 'You did.'

Luckily Mum got in first with her story about opening the door when she heard my voice. 'This is Aidan,' she said gently. 'My son.' She turned to me. 'And this is Nurse Dana.'

Even if I'd wanted to say hello and lovely to meet you I'm sure, I didn't get the chance because Dr Krinsky led Dana out, saying, 'Go and dress Isla for theatre.'

Theatre? When they'd gone, I grabbed Mum's arm. 'They're not – you're not letting them *operate* on you?'

'Course not.' Mum put her hand over mine. 'Just a few tests, nothing painful. And all in a great cause.'

I flopped down beside her on the bed, suddenly exhausted.

'What are the biggest threats to the earth, Aidan?'

'I dunno.' I rubbed my eyes. 'Climate change? War? New diseases?'

She nodded. 'And they're all happening because we're messing up the world, wasting natural resources, upsetting the balance of –'

'Who kidnapped you?' I snapped. This was hardly the time for a lecture on Doomsday.

She flinched. 'If I'd known what this was about, I'd have come willingly.'

'Couldn't risk it,' said a voice. 'We weren't sure how you'd react.'

I'd been so busy staring at Mum I hadn't noticed a figure appear in the doorway. 'You!' I gasped.

My phone burped. 'Low battery' it said on the screen. Oh no. If I turned it off, I'd miss Aidan's messages. I texted.

My battery's going. Call me NOW

I laid the phone gently on my lap, as if that would help it save energy. Should I use it up by calling the guards? But what would I tell them — that my friend was trespassing on government property? That was the only proven crime so far; the rest was guesswork. And even if we were right, and the guards did find trouble inside, they could also find a part-dragon. Then the secret would be out and I'd be to blame.

I leaned against a tree trunk. The rain tapped in the darkness. My back ached. My ankle throbbed. Cold crawled into my bones.

A FEW ANSWERS AND A
LOT MORE QUESTIONS

'Yes, Aidan. Me.' Mr Pardoe gave a tight smile. Standing in the doorway in a grey suit and tie, he looked smarter than ever.

I blinked at Mum. And guess – outrageous! – what? She was smiling back at him. 'How are you *OK* with this, Mum?'

'Oh, calm down.' Mr Pardoe folded his arms. 'We had a little scuffle back at your house, that's all. A few flames at the garden gate. But the fire extinguisher and chloroform sorted things out.' He brushed his sleeve, as if clearing off their remains. 'Then some tape on her mouth. For her own safety, obviously.'

Drugged? Gagged? 'You complete –' I got up from the bed and took a step towards him, though I had no idea what I was going to do.

'Aidan.' I felt Mum's hand on my shoulder. 'Hear us out.' She came between me and Mr Pardoe. 'Yes, I was terrified at first. I woke up when we got here and managed to claw the tape off my mouth. And yes, I started the fire in the woods. But when I met Dr Krinsky and he explained . . . oh, Aidan.' She laid a hand on my cheek. 'It's the greatest honour of my life to be here, using my gift. That's what Dr Krinsky calls it.'

Mr Pardoe made a humphy noise, suggesting that *he* certainly didn't.

I scowled. 'How did you find out about Mum?'

'I had a hunch the first time I met you.' He smirked, looking exactly like his son for a second. 'It's not often you see steam rising from cheeks on a cool September morning.' So he *had* spotted Mum's flare-up on my first day at school! 'I couldn't work out what was wrong with her at first,' he said, 'but I knew there was a problem.'

Wrong with her? Problem? It was one thing for me to think those things. But to hear them coming from his mouth? How dare he! I felt a rush of something hot and fierce and new. Pride – in my brave, *gifted* mother, who'd risked her own safety so that I could go to school and make friends.

Friends. What a joke! 'So that's why Phil was nice on my second day,' I said. 'You made him invite me round, so that I'd invite him back and you could find out more.' I frowned. 'But I don't get it. What *did* you find?'

'Oh come on. Gloves indoors? Eczema? The sudden phone call? I've done enough health inspections to know when there's something to hide. *And* where to look.'

My brain was overheating. He'd lost me again.

'I phoned a colleague in Waste Management and found out the rubbish collection time for your road. I arranged for his lads to keep your bin contents separate and deliver them to me.'

I put my hand over my mouth. I'd taken the bin out on Monday evening.

'On Tuesday morning I sorted through it myself.' Mr Pardoe ran his thumbs daintily across his fingertips. 'Disgusting. But fruitful. Because let's say the scales fell from my eyes.' He sniggered.

More of the puzzle slotted into place. Hadn't Phil said the American – Dr Krinsky – had visited on Wednesday? The envelope he'd emptied on to his palm, the doctor's excitement, the tests he said he'd run . . . Mr Pardoe must have found some of Mum's scales in the bin!

'But how did you know what they were?' I said. 'Mum's the only person in the world with dragon scales.' Again that unfamiliar rush of pride.

'It's *because* Dr Krinsky couldn't identify them that he suspected. And as for your mum being unique, don't be so sure.' Mr Pardoe wrinkled his nose. 'The way things are going, I'm beginning to think there are mutants everywhere.'

'What?' This was like cutting off one of the

Hydra's heads: for every question he answered, two more sprang up.

He batted his hand as if swatting a fly. 'I have work to do.'

'You'll get ten years for kidnapping her!'

'In ten years, young man, the world will be thanking me.' He turned and went off down the corridor, his shoes smacking the tiles as if they'd been very naughty.

'*Powering off,*' said my phone. *Shutting down.* And it did.

'Now what?' I whispered into the darkness.

'Good question,' it answered. (Actually, it said, *Hssh tpp fpp,* and other strange words in the language of rain falling through trees.)

I swallowed down the panic wriggling up my throat. There were two options. The first was to press the intercom again. But if that woman came out, she wouldn't fall for the Troy trick a second time. She'd either turn me away or get me inside too, which would be no use to Aidan or his mum.

The second option was to go back to Boonkilly, find a phone and call the gardaí. And if they found a trespassing boy and a part-dragon woman? Well, living Mooneys were better than . . .

I reached for my rucksack, then Aidan's, and hauled myself up. Pain spiked in my left ankle. I bit my lip and hobbled on to what I hoped was the path.

FUEL FOR THOUGHT

Mum took my hand and sat me back down on the bed. 'What Mr Pardoe means,' she said, perching next to me, 'is that I'm helping Dr Krinsky to solve the world's fuel problems. We all want faster cars, warmer houses, smarter technology. That'll use up coal and gas and oil that have taken millions of years to form. They could run out in a few decades.'

'So? We can use other things, like nuclear power.'

She shook her head. 'I'm no expert, but I've seen the news. Chernobyl, Japan – too many accidents already.'

'Water power? Solar?' Miss Burkitt and her Green Schools would be proud of me.

'Dr Krinsky says they're not enough. Without other energy sources, the human race will starve or freeze to death. And that's where I come in.' Her eyes glowed like jade.

'You mean,' I said slowly, 'he wants to use your

fire-breathing? But how? The gas inside you is enough to heat a teapot, not the whole world!'

'Imagine more gas,' she said, 'and millions of little worlds.'

I looked at her blankly.

'The doctor's developed a new kind of bean. It grows quickly, tastes good and produces loads of gas. The problem is how to harness that gas to use as fuel. And I'm the solution.'

I stared at her. I was beginning to understand.

'By looking at my anatomy, and the chemistry that happens inside me, he'll be able to replicate it. Then it can be installed in other people, so we're all walking fuel sources, able to store and light our own gas.'

I could feel my eyeballs taking over my face. 'So we'd all breathe fire?'

Mum smiled. 'Think how it would help the world's energy problems. If everyone could produce heat and light, they could warm a room at the very least. And there's huge potential for transport and industry. Dr Krinsky's working on all that. It's in the early stages, and I'm the key to everything.'

I put my hands on my head and tried to make sense of it all. 'But if it's so brilliant, why the secrecy?'

She tucked a strand of hair behind her ears. 'Dr Krinsky has backing at the highest international level. He's got to keep it under wraps for now. Imagine if criminals got hold of this. There'd be terrorists and maniacs breathing fire.'

I must have looked as dazed as I felt because she laid a hand on my knee. 'For the first time in my life, Aidan, I'm proud to be part-dragon. For the first time I can see a purpose in being born this way. Isn't it wonderful?'

Of course it was – for her and the whole world too. So why was my stomach churning like a slushy maker? All I could think of was Mr Pardoe in his suit and tie, breathing fire from his mean little mouth. And I couldn't bear it. Come to think of it, I couldn't bear to think of *anyone* doing it apart from Mum. Dr Krinsky had called it a gift. Well, it was *her* gift. All these years of protecting it, suffering for it, and now it would be available to everyone. All her specialness down the drain; she'd just be another run-of-the-mill fire-breather.

I knew I was being stupid and selfish. She'd always longed to fit in. And what better way than by sharing her power, making it a normal part of human behaviour, like laughing or sneezing? Tiredness must have been muddling my brain. I put a zip on my mouth and my head on her shoulder.

She stroked my hair. 'You must be starving. How about supper?' I lifted my head and nodded. 'But first I want you to meet some people.'

She stood up and led me out of the room. We went back along the corridor to the door of the room where I'd seen the man sleeping. Mum knocked.

'Come in, yes.' As we did the man sat up, pressing his knuckles into the mattress. 'Who . . .?' He stared at me. 'I did not know the visitors could come.' He spoke in a soft accent I didn't recognise. He swung his legs round to get off the bed and drew a sharp breath.

Mum raised a hand. 'Don't get up, Nikos. I want you to meet my son, Aidan. He was so worried, he came all the way here by train and bus.' She patted my arm proudly.

Nikos's brown eyes went wide. 'How you find us? How you get in?'

I shrugged. He looked like a cool person, but then so had Phil once upon three weeks ago.

'Ah.' He nodded. 'You are right to be careful.' He eased himself back on the bed. 'But Dr Krinsky is not happy, I think?'

'Not at first,' Mum said. 'But he's OK now. And he let me tell Aidan why we're here.'

'We?' Nikos frowned at her.

'I mean me. I didn't say a word about you. But you're safe to tell him. He's signed the Official Secrets form. And he's kept *my* secret all his life.'

'Tell me what?' A fizz went through me, as if someone had opened a can of Sprite in my chest. Nikos pressed his lips together.

'I promise,' Mum said. 'You can trust Aidan completely.'

But when he told me, I didn't even trust my own ears.

I stumbled down through the woods. I could just about make out the path in the fuzzy moonlight, or rather I could make out the black bulks of trees either side. The rain was stopping. Night rustled and creaked around me, as if some hidden machine was cranking out the darkness.

'Owwww!' My ankle gave way for the hundredth time. Mud squeezed over the tops of my trainers. Every bit of me was wet with rain or tears.

ANOTHER MYTHING LINK

'Wings?' I said for the third time. For the third time Nikos nodded.

'But.' I swallowed. 'How?'

Mum took my hand. 'How do I breathe fire? How do I have scales? Because there are dragon genes in my family.'

I frowned at Nikos. 'So there are bird genes in yours?'

He shook his head.

'Bat genes? Flying fish? Giant beetles? *What?*' I hadn't meant to sound so rude. 'Sorry.' I realised how Charlotte must have felt – and how well she'd handled it – the first time she saw Mum breathe fire.

Charlotte. A stone turned in my stomach. If only she were here. Especially when Nikos said, 'A horse. I have inside me the gene of Pegasus.'

Pegasus. The name flew round my head like . . . 'The winged horse,' I murmured. 'From Ancient Greece. But that's only a –'

'Legend,' Mum finished. 'Just like dragons, eh?'

Even if I'd known what to say, my mouth wasn't working.

'I am Greek,' said Nikos. 'Some long time ago, the genes of the Pegasus meet the genes of my family. I do not know how.'

'Aidan has a theory,' Mum said, 'that dragons were a missing link in evolution. Perhaps winged horses too?'

'Perhaps.' Nikos gave a little shrug then scrunched his face.

'Are you OK?' Mum stepped towards him.

He waved a hand. 'Fine, only sore. Dr Krinsky, he pull out some feathers for test.'

Feathers? How I longed to grab his smock and yank it over his head. I imagined huge milk-white wings folded neatly against his back like origami.

'Why is he testing you? Why are you here?' As soon as I'd said it, I knew the answer. 'Flying! He wants all humans to fly.'

Nikos nodded. 'My bones are light, my feathers are strong. Strong enough for carry a horse. When doctor can – how you say? – repeat my wings . . .'

'Replicate,' said Mum. 'Copy.'

'Yes, copy – then all people can fly. No more planes, no need for fuel, no more pollution.'

'Brilliant, isn't it?' Mum sat next to Nikos on the bed. 'And I'll tell you what's even more brilliant, at least for me.' She reached out a hand towards

Nikos's shoulder but, when he flinched, pulled it back. 'To make a new friend. Someone who knows what it's like to live with a secret that makes you feel like God's mistake.'

'Until now,' he said. 'Now we are God's answer. And I too have found a friend.'

'Two,' said Mum. Now she couldn't help touching his arm. 'One of them extra-special.'

He smiled shyly. 'Aidan has met Isla?'

Mum shook her head. 'She's gone for tests.'

'Is that the lady I saw in the other room? Why is she wearing that . . . ?' The question died on my lips. Because suddenly I knew what was under her hat.

The trees gave way to open track. The track turned to tarmac. The barn on my left, then the farmhouse and cottages — and, wow, what a whoosh of relief to make out the houses, solid and safe in the slippery moonlight. I limped to the end of the village and stopped outside Geraghty's Store 'n' More. A light was on in an upstairs window. I paused by the petrol pump and rehearsed my lines. Then I reached out and pressed the bell.

FANTASTIC

The kitchen was down the corridor beyond Mum's room. It was pretty basic, with a fridge, a microwave and a sink. I sat at the table while Mum toasted a cheese sandwich by wrapping it in foil and breathing on it.

Nikos stood and clapped. 'Your mother is magic,' he said as she bathed the package in wispy blue flame.

'That makes two of you,' I said.

I was just about to ask to see his wings when the kitchen door opened. Standing in the doorway was the young woman I'd seen when I first came down the corridor. Her pretty face was as pale as her turban, which I could see now was a bandage. The cone came to a point about twenty centimetres above her head. She saw me and stepped back, looking as queasy as I felt. There were red stains at the bottom of the bandage. Nikos sprang forward and took her arm. He led her gently to the table and sat her in a chair.

'Isla,' Mum said. 'This is Aidan, my son.'

Isla blinked at me with grey, bemused eyes.

'Are you OK?' Mum reached her arm across the table.

Isla put an elbow on the table and rested her head on her palm. 'Just a wee bit woozy.'

'Aidan's come to visit me,' Mum said, vaguely enough, I hoped, to ward off any questions about how I'd got in.

Nikos pulled up another chair. He turned it round and sat down, leaning forward against the chair back so that his own sore back was free. 'What they do?'

Isla gave me a nervous glance. 'Some tests.' She had a Scottish accent, soft as a song.

'It's OK.' Mum wiggled her claws. 'Aidan's grown up with me. You can tell him.'

'She doesn't have to,' I blurted out. 'I know what's under that bandage. A unicorn horn.'

Isla squealed. Her hand flew to her head, as if trying to hide the turban. It was like a spider trying to hide a traffic cone. She drew a hissy breath as her fingertips touched the dressing. 'How d'ye know?'

'A man with Pegasus wings? A dragon mum? Why not?' I hadn't meant to be flippant, but tears came into Isla's eyes.

'Go easy, love,' Mum murmured. 'You can imagine, with *that* on her head Isla's had to hide away completely. She's not used to new people, not

173

even Nikos and me. And we understand better than anyone.' The way Nikos reached for Isla's hand, he did more than understand.

But I was struggling to understand anything. 'Does that mean there are more people out there with mythical genes? What about mermaids and centaurs and . . .' I trailed off as trolls and werewolves rampaged through my mind.

Mum put a hand on my arm. 'All we know is that Dr Krinsky found us.'

And what a find! Dragon, Pegasus and unicorn genes. Impossible, unthinkable, unbelievable – except that here they were, sitting round the table. 'Fire-breathing, flying and . . .' I tried to remember what I knew about unicorns. Not much: I'm a boy. 'What does he want from your horn, Isla?'

She sat up straight. 'Medicine. Ground-up unicorn horn cures diseases.'

'So he cut out a piece to test it?' I sucked my teeth. 'That must've hurt.'

Isla gave a wincy nod. 'But it's worth it. Dr Krinsky's going to analyse the chemistry of my alicorn. That's the proper name for a unicorn horn.' Her wince relaxed into a proud little smile. 'Imagine if drug companies could reproduce it artificially. Imagine if one day there was a single pill to cure all diseases. No more deaths from cancer or AIDS. Fantastic.'

I did imagine. And it was fantastic. So fantastic that a strange panic fluttered inside me. Fire-breathing humans who could fly and survive all disease? It felt like too much too fast. We'd taken hundreds of thousands of years to become this wingless, air-breathing, disease-prone species called human. How would we cope with such sudden, massive change?

I could hardly ask that question in front of these shining faces. So instead I unwrapped my foil and bit into cheesy, toasty bliss.

'Now calm down, dear,' said Mrs Geraghty (I guessed her name from the shop sign). 'And start again.' She sat me down at a table in the back room of her store. 'Slowly this time.'

Oh, the relief as the weight lifted off my ankle! 'My family,' I said through chattering teeth. 'They're lost in the woods up that hill. I need to call the guards.'

She sat opposite me. Her friendly face went all frowny. 'What in heaven's name are they doing up there at nine o'clock at night?'

Keep it as simple as possible, I told myself — which wasn't very. 'We're camping in the woods. Remember when my brother and I came here this afternoon, you said that IRC place was private? Well, I dared him to go there at night and ring the intercom. A lady came out and shouted at him. He ran off. I was watching from the trees. I couldn't find him so I went back to the tent. Mum and Dad went looking and they got lost too.'

Aidan's right about me being a rubbish liar. Even I wouldn't have believed me. I burst into tears to cover my bad acting. After the last few hours, that bit wasn't acting at all. 'It's all my fault.'

She squeezed my arm. 'Shhh, dear, you're OK. Sounds a bit strange, though, I must say. Are you sure of all this?'

I sobbed louder. 'Course I am. I was there. You have to believe me.'

'We do, so,' said a man who'd come down a staircase in the corner of the room. Mr Geraghty (I guessed again) had a bald, reddish head like Mars. 'At least, we have to act as if we do. Because if it is true, we'd feel terrible doing nothing.' He came over to Mrs Geraghty. 'And if it isn't,' he said, patting her shoulder, 'then it's not our problem, Maura. I'll ring Liam.'

'You must be freezing, dear.' Mrs Geraghty took my hand.

'I'm fine,' I said, shivery-snivelling. 'Who's Liam?'

'Sergeant Barry,' Mr Geraghty said. 'Friend of mine. Head of the nearest garda station in Rathboyle. It's a twenty-minute drive, mind. He won't thank you for calling him out on a wild goose chase.' He raised his eyebrows, as if giving me a chance to come clean.

'Can I talk to him on the phone?'

'Leave it to Joe.' Mrs Geraghty was in mammy mode. 'Let's get you into some dry clothes. Sorry, dear, what's your name again?'

I remembered just in time. 'Cassandra.'

TOOBS

'Bedtime,' Mum said as I finished my second toasted sandwich. Isla said she'd clear up the kitchen and Nikos said he'd help her.

Mum winked. 'Let's leave them to it.' We went back along the corridor past a bathroom, which I used, and a door with a sign that said 'Administration Office'. Reaching Mum's room, I stopped. 'What are those double doors?' I pointed to the far end of the corridor.

'The medical wing. That's where Dr Krinsky does the tests.'

My throat went tight. 'Will you be OK, Mum? It looked painful for Nikos and Isla.'

'Like a wasp sting.' She said it lightly but there was a wobble in her voice. 'Best thing for you is to get a good night's sleep. Me too, once Dr Krinsky's finished. I'll be grand tomorrow.' Again that wobble.

I followed her into her room and over to the bed. 'Wasp stings don't make you bleed. And anyway, you're different. Wings and horns are on the outside. Your fire-breathing stuff's inside. Won't he have to cut into you?'

She pulled back the duvet. 'Just for a tiny tissue sample. Doctors do biopsies all the time. And like Isla said, it's a small price to pay.'

I sat on the bed. 'Where will you sleep? Please stay here.'

'Sure.' Mum plumped up the pillow. 'I'll ask Dana to put a mattress on the floor when I'm done.'

My chest felt heavy, as if I'd swallowed a sponge. 'I'm not sleeping till you're back from the tests.'

'At least come and rest.'

I lay on the bed. It sounds babyish but it was good having Mum there to tuck me in like when I was little. Everything about this place, from the cold clean smell to the people and their plans, was so very strange. Thank goodness for the familiar loveliness of her face and the sweet, toasty smell as she bent to kiss my cheek.

'It might have made things tricky,' she said, 'but I'm glad you're with me now, darling.'

'Me too.' That was only half a lie. I *was* glad about being with her, but not about the now. If only it was Monday and we could go home.

Despite my determination to stay awake I must have dozed off because I was woken by voices. I sat bolt upright. Dr Krinsky stood in the doorway.

Mum was sitting at the end of the bed. 'Go back

to sleep, love. I'll see you soon.' She stood up.

My stomach pinched tight. 'You won't hurt her?' I said to the doctor. It was meant to be an order but it came out as a question.

His smile blazed into the room. 'Not in a million years.' He came over to the bed. 'Look, son, I know how much you care about Mom.'

Son? Better than kiddo at least.

'And I see why. We only met two days ago, but she's a great lady.'

I nodded fiercely. 'So why did Mr Pardoe called her a mutant?'

Dr Krinsky brought his fingertips to his lips, as if praying. 'Derek Pardoe isn't the most, let's say, *imaginative* man. He loves order and control. Anything that messes up his neat little life, well, he wants to get rid of it.' The doctor tutted. 'That's why I chose him. He was the right man to track Mom down and bring her here – out of the way, as he saw it. His job's done now. She's in safe hands.' One of those hands reached over and patted the duvet over my knees. 'What I'm saying, son, is that from a personal *and* a professional point of view, the last thing I'd do is hurt her.' He crouched by the bed. 'To be scientifically blunt, we need her in perfect working order so we can see how she breathes fire.'

'So you're not going to take a sample, like you did from the others?'

'No. I just need to look inside Mom. I'm gonna put a tiny toob through her nose and down her throat. Then I can look at her bronchi, the toobs that carry air into the lungs.'

When I'd worked out what 'toobs' were, I said, 'Will it hurt?' I didn't want to sound whiney but that was all my voice was offering.

'Not a bit. Dana will give Mom an anaesthetic. She won't feel a thing.' He fixed me with his sky-blue gaze. 'I know this is hard, Aidan.' It was the first time he'd used my name, the first time it felt he was taking me seriously. 'You see why we didn't want you involved? But you have to trust me. You're part of the team now.'

His eyes were so clear and kind. Relief rose inside me. 'Who else is there, apart from Mr Pardoe and Dana?'

The doctor leaned over and patted my arm as if congratulating me. 'You're in select company. Just a few top US government staff, and a handful of European agents. Like Derek, they all work for town or city councils and deal with the public. We chose them for their discretion and sharp eyes. They report anyone who looks or behaves unusually, who might have something to hide, anatomically speaking.'

I thought of Mr Pardoe spotting Mum's steaming cheeks on my first day at school. I pictured his European colleagues: French Derec in a beret,

German Dirk in lederhosen, flamenco-dancing Dereco from Spain. 'Are they in every country?'

Dr Krinsky shook his head. 'We've targeted the ones where a certain mythical creature is a big shot in the folklore. I figured the stories may have started because the creature once really existed there.' He grinned. 'And I figured right.'

No surprise there. I couldn't imagine Dr Krinsky ever figuring wrong.

'Take Scotland,' he said. 'Two unicorns on its coat of arms, and whaddya know, that's where we found Isla. Then Greece, home of the Pegasus legend and Nikos. I gotta say, though,' he touched Mum's arm, 'you were a surprise, Shauna. I expected leprechauns or giants in Ireland, not dragons.' His hand moved under her elbow. 'Until you told me yesterday about your Welsh blood. Then it made sense.' He guided her to the door. 'Sleep tight, Aidan. Mom'll be back before you know it, OK?'

As he turned and smiled at me, it was OK. But the minute the door closed behind them, my confidence drained away. His presence was so powerful, so bright: a torch that held me in its beam. But when he left the light left with him, leaving a lump of black fear that twisted in my gut. Even if he could copy Mum's fire-breathing mechanism, how did he know it would work inside others? Her gift was in her genes. Her body was designed for it, but other bodies weren't. I'd heard of people spontaneously combusting, their insides catching fire with no obvious trigger. How much more likely if there *was* a trigger: a device implanted to make them breathe fire.

I lay on my back and stared at the ceiling. Questions crashed round my head. What about the environment? If millions of people breathed fire, wouldn't that produce more greenhouse gases and speed up global warming, so we'd all die anyway? Did Dr Krinsky have scientists working on that problem? What about other doctors? For such an important project, shouldn't there be a medical team behind him, with lung and back and nose and throat and bone and skin and blood specialists? He convinced Mum and Nikos and Isla, swept them up in his dream. And no wonder. After a lifetime of shame, they at last felt proud to be different.

But I wasn't different. And I wasn't swept up.

I pushed back the duvet and slipped off the bed. Leaving my shoes where I'd thrown them on the floor, I crept in socky silence to the door.

I was on my third cup of tea when the shop bell rang. Mr Geraghty went to get it. He came back followed by a guard.

'Maura.' The guard took off his hat. He had a big, red face and shoulders as wide as the doorway.

'Liam,' she said. 'You'll have a cuppa.'

'Oh, I won't say no, so I won't.' He sat at the table while she poured, then wrapped a hand round the steaming cup; his fingers were too thick to fit through the handle. He tilted his face back and gulped the whole lot in one go.

'Now young lady,' he said, though I felt more like a young gorilla in Mr Geraghty's woolly brown sweater that hung to my knees, 'I'm Sergeant Barry. Joe's told me your story.' He had a deep booming voice. Good. That would sound impressive over the intercom; they'd let him in no problem. What *was* a problem was persuading him to press it in the first place. I'd have to tell more of the truth. But not in front of the Geraghtys. I owed it to Mrs Mooney to limit the possible number of dragon–discoverers.

'I have to warn you,' he said, 'that wasting garda time is a criminal offence.'

'I'm not.' I repeated the lost–in–the–woods story. I'd update it in the car when it was just the two of us.

Except, as we headed for the door, Mr Geraghty said, 'Leave a few scones out, Maura. Dare say we'll be peckish when we get back.'

THE STORE ROOM

I crept along the corridor to the administration office. I put my ear to the door but all I could hear was my heart drumming like rain on a tent. My hand closed round the cold metal handle. There were four things that could go wrong:

1. The door wouldn't open.
2. The door would open and there'd be someone inside.
3. There'd be no one inside but no phone either.
4. I'd forget to breathe.

One out of four wasn't bad. Five seconds later I remembered to breathe again. I reached for the phone on the desk. My hand stopped. If only I'd memorised Charlotte's number. I called the only one I knew apart from Mum's.

After seven rings came Gramps's sleepy voice. 'Hello?'

'It's Aidan,' I whispered.

'Sorry, who?'

'Aidan. Listen, Gramps –'

'Aidan? How are you? Why are you whispering?'

'I'm in this place with Mum, and –'

The receiver flew from my grasp. A hand slammed it down on the phone.

'What the hell?!' Dana spun me round. 'Who are you calling?' She shook my shoulders. 'What did you say?'

I stared at her, my lips clamped. She slapped my face. 'Dr Krinsky should nevera let you stay.' She grabbed my arms and pulled me towards the door. 'D'you want to ruin everything?' She was even stronger than she looked. I yanked and twisted and kicked but she didn't even flinch. She dragged me down the corridor to a door beyond the kitchen. She slid a bolt back, opened the door and shoved me through. I stumbled forward. The door slammed. I heard the bolt slide across.

I stood frozen in the darkness. There was a faint lemony smell. I stretched out my arms and circled them in front. My left hand met a wall. I ran my fingers up and down until – thank goodness – they found a switch. The light came on.

I was in a big, square, windowless room: a kind of store-room-cum-laundry. Shelves along the left-hand wall were piled with towels and bed linen. Against the right-hand wall was a stack of chairs and a narrow wardrobe thing, which I guessed was a broom cupboard. A washing machine stood against the back wall. Next to it were more shelves, on which stood household cleaning stuff: washing powder, lemon multipurpose spray, cloths and dusters.

I sat on the floor, drew up my legs and put my head on my knees. *Great. Damn great. Damn and in fact bloody great.*

The garda car slowed as we approached the woods. Sergeant Barry let out a long, noisy breath. 'Now, Cassandra.' He turned to me in the back. 'Where did you say your tent was?' He glanced at Mr Geraghty in the passenger seat. They clearly didn't believe a word of my story.

'I'm not sure in the dark. Somewhere at the top of the hill, near that research place.'

He tutted. 'Not too near, I hope. They need their privacy.'

'Who do?' I asked as casually as I could.

He turned forward again and gripped the wheel with his meaty hands. 'The government.'

Which, on a scale of one to helpful, was chicken poop.

COMPANY

It wasn't much of a plan. But it was all I could think of. I stood to the left of the door, so that when it opened I'd be hidden. In my right hand was a broom I'd found in the cupboard. It was simple enough – stick out the broom when Dana came back, trip her up and run out.

If Dana came back. What if she told everyone that I'd decided to go home, and just left me here for ever? I wouldn't put it past her.

So when I heard quick footsteps, and the creak of the bolt sliding back, I felt almost grateful. I clutched my weapons and held my breath.

The door opened. I shoved out the broom . . . and jerked it back.

'Mum?!'

Behind her came Isla. The door slammed. The bolt slid across.

Mum's hands and claws were wrapped in bandages like giant mittens. Her face was pale.

My mouth went dry. 'What's he done to you, Mum?'

'Exactly what he said. A bronchoscopy – a tube down my throat to look at my lungs. And he took some scales from my hands to analyse, that's all. I'm OK.' Her eyes glittered with anger, or fear, I couldn't tell which. 'Who did you phone? And why?'

'Gramps. I – I don't trust Dr Krinsky, Mum.'

'Well how do you think he feels about you?! He's furious, says you've risked the whole project.'

'But I didn't tell Gramps anything.'

'You think he'll believe that? He says he's got to speed things up now, do the tests he needs before the public gets wind of anything. That's why we're in here too. He can't risk anyone delaying things, even accidentally.'

'What about Nikos?'

'He's gone for more tests,' Isla said. Her eyes were huge and scared.

I bit the knuckle of my forefinger. I'd made things a million times worse. I hadn't even managed to tell Gramps where we were. There was nothing he could do – and nothing Dr Krinsky couldn't.

Sergeant Barry parked the car in front of the IRC. He twisted round in the driver's seat. 'You wait here, Cassandra. Can't have you lost as well, so we can't. Where did your brother run off?'

I pointed vaguely left along the fence.

'And the tent. Any idea what direction?'

I pointed vaguely right.

He nodded. 'I'll look for the boy, Joe. You check out the tent. See you back here in half an hour.' Mr Geraghty nodded. He got out of the car and closed the door.

'Actually, Sergeant Barry,' I said, 'I need to tell you something.'

He turned from the front again. 'Do you now, young lady?' From the arch of his eyebrows, I could tell he wasn't surprised. 'How about the truth?'

HEALING

Isla and I took down three chairs from the stack by the wall. We sat in silence.

At last Mum said, 'I'm sure Nikos will join us soon.' She reached out a bandaged hand and touched Isla's arm lightly. 'Then Dr Krinsky will have everything he needs and we'll be free to go.'

I'd almost managed to believe that when we heard scuffly footsteps and angry voices in the corridor. The bolt slid back. We all jumped up as a hospital trolley trundled in and came to a stop in front of our chairs. Dana followed, almost crashing into it as someone shoved her from behind. The door slammed.

And Isla screamed.

Nikos was on the trolley. He lay on his front with his face to one side. His skin was dull and blotchy like brown bread. He was sleeping. It wasn't a peaceful nap. His mouth was pinched and he took quick, shallow breaths. His fists clenched by his sides, as if pain was bypassing his mind and racking his body. His poor body.

Isla reached out a hand and held it over the trolley, not daring to touch. A white sheet covered his back. Two red circles were spreading slowly over two terrible bumps at the tops of his shoulder blades.

I opened my mouth but nothing came out.

'His wings.' Mum's voice was flat. She looked at Dana with unblinking eyes.

Dana raised her hands as if in prayer. Her wrists were handcuffed. Bending over the trolley, she stroked Nikos's hair with her fingertips. The movement was amazingly gentle. 'I swear to God,' she whispered, 'I had no idea.'

Nikos moaned.

'Shhh,' Dana murmured, 'it's OK. Go back to sleep, there.' She drew a fingertip across his forehead, again so very gently. He closed his eyes.

'Dr Krinsky said he was taking a tiny bone sample,' she said faintly, 'to analyse the wing skeleton. He told me to give Nikos a sedative in case it was uncomfortable. Uncomfortable?' She snorted. 'I gave him the pills. Then I went to the back room to scrub up. As I was washing my hands I heard a cry, then a . . . a snapping sound. I ran back into theatre. Dr Krinsky had a saw in one hand. And with the other, he was holding up –' She bit her lip. 'Wings.' She shook her head, as if

191

trying to empty out the memory. 'When I realised what he'd done, I flew at him.' She flinched at the dreadful accidental pun. 'He grabbed me and shouted to Pardoe to get handcuffs.'

'Didn't you – tell him – what Krinsky – had done?' My words stuttered out like water from a blocked tap.

'He saw it himself. And you think he cares? Anything to get rid of a freak.'

'And you,' Mum said quietly, 'do you agree?'

'Oh please!' Dana shook her handcuffed wrists. 'Why do you think I'm in here? Krinsky's fanatical. He'll do anything to save the human race.' She laughed harshly. 'Even mutilate humans.'

I sank down on my chair. My mother was one of those humans.

Isla, though, seemed suddenly energised. 'What am I thinking of?' She looked round the room with bright, busy eyes. 'I need something to . . .' She went to the shelves along the back wall. Rummaging through the cleaning cloths, she found two dark green scouring pads. 'Perfect.' She put a hand behind her head and began to unwind her bandage.

'Wow,' I murmured as my very first alicorn came into sight. It was pinky brown, covered in tiny silver hairs that glittered under the ceiling lights. There were two pieces of gauze at the front, stained with blood from the horn sample Dr Krinsky had taken.

When the bottom half was exposed, Isla stopped unravelling and tucked the bandage in. She took the scourers and pressed one each side of her horn. Returning to the trolley, she rubbed the pads up and down in a dry, rustly rhythm like sandpapering wood. She stared ahead, her face set tight. If she felt any pain, she wasn't going to show it.

She bent over Nikos. 'Will ye lift the sheet, Aidan? Now, hold it there.' She slipped the scourers underneath. I saw they were dusted on one side with pink powder. There was a whiff of vanilla mixed with woodsmoke. 'Now ye can fold the sheet back.' Her hands rested gently on the scourers, covering the bumps on Nikos's bare back. A shiver ran across his shoulders. She began to hum, a soft sweet sound, as if the scent had entered her voice.

Nikos gave a deep sigh. His hands unclenched by his side and his breathing slowed.

Isla smiled at me and nodded towards the back shelf. 'For your mum.'

I fetched two more scouring pads. I tried to be gentle as I rubbed them up and down the sides of her horn.

'Harder,' she urged, biting her top lip. A little cloud of pink dust rose from the pads as I took them to Mum and laid them, powder-side up, on her lap. I unwrapped her mitten bandages. There were raw red patches on the backs of her hands where the scales had been pulled out. I placed the scourers gently over them.

'Aaah,' she breathed, closing her eyes. After a minute or so, she said, 'The pain's completely gone.'

'Take a peek,' Isla said, rewinding the bandage to cover her horn. I lifted the scourers from Mum's hands. The angry redness had calmed to smooth healing scabs.

Mum flexed her claws slowly. 'Well, look at that,' she said, shaking her head in wonder.

'And look at *that*.' Dana pointed at Nikos.

His eyelids were fluttering. He gave a little snort. 'Pou eemay,' he mumbled in what must be Greek. Then his eyes opened wide. 'Where am I?'

The problem with lying is that when you do come out with the truth, it's harder to make people believe you. Especially when you have to leave out important details.

'So now you're telling me that he's not your brother but your friend,' Sergeant Barry said as we stood by the fence. 'And he sneaked into the building behind a woman who opened the gate.' (I'd left out the code-cracking details to avoid more questions.) 'And you want me to press the intercom, go inside and have a look round.'

I nodded.

'Because you think your friend's mother was kidnapped.'

'Yes.'

He scratched his big red cheek. 'But you don't know why.'

'I have an idea. But I can't say.'

He shone his torch on his watch. 'They'll all be in bed.'

'Not if they're busy doing kidnappy things, like interrogating and torturing.'

He shifted from one foot to the other.

'You'll never live it down if I'm right.'

He bounced his fist against his chin. 'We've had orders not to disturb.'

'From who?'

'Never you mind.'

'You mean you don't have a clue what's going on in there.'

He opened his mouth and closed it. He took off his hat and frowned at it. Then he nodded and put it back on, as if it had told him what to do. Handing me his torch, he stepped forward and pressed the intercom. 'Sergeant Barry here, Rathboyle gardaí.' He cleared his throat. 'Wonder if I could, ah, pop in, just to check you're OK.'

When no one answered he clapped his hands. 'Right so.' He smiled with relief. 'All in bed. We can't do any more tonight. We'll wait for Joe and go home. I'll come back at a decent hour tomorrow.'

He went back to the car. I stood by the fence with my arms folded. If only I could climb over it, I knew the door code.

ATTACK

Dana bent over the trolley. 'That's just . . .' She gasped as Nikos yawned and stirred. 'I've never seen anything . . .' The bumps at the tops of his shoulder blades were covered in smooth, shiny skin, slightly lighter than the rest of his back. She turned to Isla. 'Wound healing as well as curing diseases? You'll put us nurses out of a job.'

Isla blushed.

Nikos rolled on to his side, slowly coming round from the sedative.

A faint shriek, high and pure, came from somewhere down the corridor.

'Mr Pardoe?' Call me terrible, but I felt a whoosh of hope. 'If Dr Krinsky's hurt him too, then at least he's out of our way.'

'We need a plan,' Dana said, 'before Krinsky comes back for –' she didn't have to finish. We knew who she meant. He'd got his horn sample and his wings.

Well, I'd die before he got anything else.

'You can breathe fire on him, Mum.'

She stood up, shaking her head. 'Not in this room. There are no windows. If he comes in and I breathe fire, then he leaves and locks us in, that'll be it.'

'We'll have to wheel Nikos out on the trolley,' Isla said. 'He's not really with it yet.'

He smiled dreamily as she squeezed his hand.

There were footsteps in the corridor, quick and sharp. I took the broom from the wall, ran behind the door and crouched down. As it opened, I stuck out the handle. But instead of tripping over it, Dr Krinsky bent down, grabbed the end and snatched up the broom in one easy movement. He strode across the room towards Mum. Behind him came – oh no – Mr Pardoe, looking as neat and unhurt as ever. He carried a fire extinguisher.

Dana tried to block the doctor's way but he jabbed the broom handle like a lance into her stomach. She yelped and bent forward, clutching her middle. I shoved the trolley at him. He stumbled backwards.

Nikos rolled on to his back and pushed himself up on his elbows. 'What?' he said blearily. Isla cowered behind him, her arms round his shoulders.

Mr Pardoe darted round the trolley towards Mum. She backed against the washing machine in the corner.

'Don't even think of it,' he said, pointing the fire extinguisher hose at her mouth. I ran to the back wall, grabbed the bottle of lemon spray from the shelf and squirted him in the face. He squealed and dropped the fire extinguisher, screwing his fists into his eyes. I reached for the extinguisher. But Dr Krinsky got there first. Dana straightened up and lunged at him.

'No!' I shouted as he whacked the fire extinguisher against her head. There was a horrible thud. She fell to the ground. I threw down the now empty spray bottle and charged at Dr Krinsky's back. He whirled round and rammed the extinguisher into my stomach, punching the air out of me. I crash-sat on the floor. Pain knifed up my spine. Dr Krinsky rushed at Mum, fire extinguisher in one hand, broom in the other. She raised her arms to fend him off. Only then did she – and he – seem to remember what was at the end of them. Unbandaged.

'Aaaagh!' he roared, twisting his head away as she clawed his face. Three red lines blossomed down each cheek. He dropped the broom.

Mr Pardoe came behind him. Lemony tears streamed down his face. He grasped Mum's wrists, but not before she'd slashed the front of his perfect grey jacket.

'Don't hurt her,' Krinsky snarled. 'Not yet.' He spun Mum round and wrenched her arms behind her. Mr Pardoe pinned them against her back while he took a pair of handcuffs from his lab-coat pocket and clamped her wrists.

I stood up and ran at him again. He gripped my arm and practically threw me across the room. I didn't stand a chance against his strength.

But someone did. Someone who'd woken up completely. Nikos had slipped off the trolley and pulled off one of his slippers. He raised his pyjama leg and kicked Dr Krinsky.

I gasped. Because it wasn't a foot that met the doctor's stomach. It was a hard, sharp hoof.

The doctor roared and doubled over. Nikos kicked again. But as his leg rose, Mr Pardoe kicked his other one from behind, sending Nikos sprawling on to his back. Isla rushed over. Dr Krinsky lay on the floor, hugging the fire extinguisher to his stomach and moaning. And now Isla – gentle Isla who wouldn't hurt a fly – lowered her head and charged.

But Mr Pardoe was too quick. Like a bullfighter, he skipped aside, caught the tip of her horn, yanked it away and sent her smacking into the wall. He seized Mum's arm and dragged her through the door. I stumbled after them into the corridor.

Now out of the store room, Mum played her ace. A flame burst from her mouth, catching the edge of Mr Pardoe's sleeve. He shrieked and shook his arm madly. But before I could pull her away, a cloud of foam hit his sleeve, dousing the flame. Dr Krinsky must have had a six-pack made of steel because he'd staggered to his feet. Clutching the fire extinguisher, he came through the door, slammed it and drew the bolt across.

Mum breathed at him, but again he quenched the flame, spraying her lips with foam. As she gasped for breath, he whisked a pill from his pocket. He stuffed it into her mouth and pushed her head back.

'Spit it out!' I yelled. But she'd already swallowed it.

She twisted her head and shouted, 'Run, Aidan!'

I did. But not towards the front door. I hurled myself at Dr Krinsky.

He turned and clamped both my wrists in his right hand. His grip was steely strong. 'Tape!' he snapped.

Mr Pardoe took a roll of silver tape and a scalpel from his pocket. He cut off a strip and stuck it across Mum's mouth. It must have been fire resistant because no more flames escaped. He leaned across her and, with the help of Dr Krinsky, wound it round my wrists three times before cutting the end. The more I wriggled my hands, the more it dug in, stiff and tight.

Dr Krinsky dropped the fire extinguisher: no need for it now. The two men shoved us down the corridor towards the medical wing, Mum snorting smoke from her nostrils, me kicking and yelling my head off.

'Come on, Cassandra,' Sergeant Barry tapped my shoulder. I was still staring through the fence. Mr Geraghty was back from his wild tent chase and the guard had updated him on my story. 'Get in the car. You can come back with me first thing tomorr—'

'Shhh!' I hissed. 'What's that?'

'What?' He took a step towards the fence.

'Shouting.' I pressed my face to the freezing steel bars of the fence. 'From inside.'

Mr Geraghty joined us. More shouting, furious and desperate. They looked at each other.

'That's my friend's voice,' I said as the shouting faded and stopped.

Sergeant Barry pressed the intercom again. 'This is Rathboyle gardaí,' he boomed. 'Open the door. Immediately.'

He took a phone from his pocket and pressed it. 'Donal?' he said. 'It's Liam. Incident at the research centre above Boonkilly. Possible kidnapping, long story. Get me back-up.'

I tugged his sleeve. 'And a ladder to climb the fence. I know how to get in the front door.'

He stared at me. Then he said into the phone, 'Send a fire engine up here.' He turned and walked away so I wouldn't hear. But Sergeant Barry's whisper was only a slightly softer boom than his normal speaking voice. 'Ambulance too, just in case.'

BREATHE!

The double doors swung shut behind us. We'd entered a huge room that seemed to be half laboratory, half surgery. It had a spooky white glow, as if everything was coated in milk. Against one wall stood shelves of bottles with complicated labels: ethyl oleate, chloro-something acid. There was a low hum, as if every piece of equipment was breathing, from the machines with screens to the big round light above the operating table.

The operating table. My stomach turned over.

At one end of the table was a metal stand with scissors, scalpels and cotton wool on top. The floor was sprinkled with Nikos's feathers.

'Sedate him, Derek.' The doctor took another pill from his pocket and handed it to Mr Pardoe. Then he bundled Mum towards the operating table. Her head lolled.

'Stay awake, Mum!' I shouted. Mr Pardoe pressed his hand over my mouth, holding the palm flat so

I couldn't bite him. I clamped my lips. A tablet slipped past my chin and dropped to the floor. I stamped it into powder.

'You wanna watch? Fine!' Dr Krinsky lifted Mum on to the table. 'But you're gonna wish you'd swallowed that pill.' He rolled Mum on to her right side. He pulled a strap out from one side of the table and over her shoulder, clipping it to the other side. He pulled another strap over her ankles, then tightened them both until she moaned in pain.

'That ain't nothing, honey.' He turned to us. 'Tie him up.'

No more 'Aidan', no more 'kiddo', just a cold, hard 'him'.

Mr Pardoe dragged me to the wall and shoved me into a chair, one of those office seats on wheels. He unrolled the tape. It screeched over my lap and under the seat, again and again. He cut the end with the scalpel. Then he pulled more tape across my chest and stuck each end to the wall. I wriggled madly but the superstrong tape stuck fast.

'I'm gonna scrub up,' Dr Krinsky said. He went to the back of the room, opened a door and disappeared to the left. Through the open door, I saw a cage on a stand. I caught my breath.

At the bottom of the cage was a bird. *His* bird. The Amazonian parrot lay like a heap of tinsel. From the wonky angle, I knew it was dead. Was that the faint shriek we'd heard while in the store room, that I thought had come from Mr Pardoe? Had this madman killed his pet in a rage?

He came out again wearing a green top and rubber gloves. He glided across to Mum, unstoppable as lava. She lay on her side, her wrists cuffed behind her, staring dully ahead.

'Wake up!' I wailed.

'Dream on,' Dr Krinsky snarled.

He beckoned to Mr Pardoe. 'Get over here. I need you, now Dana's deserted.'

'But . . .' Mr Pardoe twisted his hands together. 'I'm your link man, Leviticus, not your nurse. You know I have no medical –'

'Here!'

As Mr Pardoe came to the table, I pushed out my chest, again and again. The tape pulled tight.

'Scissors,' Dr Krinsky said. Mr Pardoe passed him a pair from the stand at Mum's feet. He cut a hole in her pyjama top, exposing a patch of skin beneath her armpit.

'No!' I yelled. 'You promised not to operate.'

The doctor spun round. His eyes were blue metal. 'And *you* promised not to contact anyone. Your phone call changed the rules.'

'But she hasn't even had an anaesthetic!'

'No need. It's all one way from here.'

The way he said it, flat and hard, I knew what he meant. Tears burst from my eyes. I wiggled my shoulders desperately. The tape stretched across my chest.

'She's zoned out. Untape her mouth,' Dr Krinsky said. 'I need her breathing freely when I open up.'

Mr Pardoe ripped the tape off her mouth leaving a red streak across her pale cheeks. Her face scrunched. She was sedated but aware of pain, the worst possible combination.

'Chlorhexidine.' The doctor held out his hand.

'W–what?' Mr Pardoe said.

'Jeez, Derek. The alcohol to clean the skin. In that bottle.' He nodded towards the stand at Mum's feet. 'It'll ruin things if the lungs come out infected.'

Lungs? Come out?

'Stop!' I screamed as Mr Pardoe passed him the bottle.

The doctor soaked a swab of cotton wool and wiped Mum's skin. Mr Pardoe replaced the alcohol on the stand. My brain turned to ice. Mum stared ahead, a ghost with empty eyes.

Empty eyes. A crack slit the ice. *Ghost.* The crack widened. *Alcohol.* A memory slipped through.

I took the biggest breath of my life.

'MUM – GHOST CAKE – *BREEATHE!*'

Maybe it was the pitch of my voice. Maybe it was the cold of the alcohol on her skin. Or maybe the memory itself hopped like a Halloween frog into her swampy brain. Whatever – something got through to her.

The next few seconds were so all-at-once they take a hundred times longer to describe, but here goes. Mum opened her mouth. I pushed my socky feet against the floor and gave a massive shove forward. The tape ripped free from the wall. With a kind of flicking movement between my heels and toes, I wheeled across to the stand at her feet. I raised my taped wrists like a bat and whacked the bottle of alcohol off the table. It smashed at the men's feet. Mum breathed out a perfectly timed, perfectly aimed flame. There was an everlasting second of stillness. Then the world exploded.

The men spun round yelling. Flames tickled their ankles. I wheeled across to the shelves and swept my arms along, knocking off a row of bottles. They crashed to the floor, spilling a hundred lonely chemicals just itching to meet a friendly flame.

Mr Pardoe shrieked and rushed to the side of the room. His socks were on fire. He grabbed a fire extinguisher from the wall and squirted his ankles. Then he turned the nozzle on Dr Krinsky whose trousers were alight. Flames ate the bottom of his lab coat and danced up his sleeves. He hopped and roared to the back room, ran through and slammed the door. Mr Pardoe raced back to Mum who was still breathing flames. He forced the nozzle into her mouth.

'NO!' I shouted as he squeezed the trigger once, twice, three times. Then he ran to the entrance doors and crashed through to the corridor.

I shot across to Mum, dodging the fires on the floor. I grasped the nozzle with my bound hands and pulled the extinguisher out of her mouth. Foam bubbled from her lips. Coughing in the fumes, I pushed myself along the table to the stand at her feet. I grabbed a pair of scissors with my clumsy fingers and cut through the tape round my wrists. With my hands free, I sliced the tape across my lap and broke free of the chair. Flames danced from the puddles on the floor: reds and yellows, weird blues and greens. Sweat blurred my eyes. My brain swam.

Somehow I found a switch at the side of the trolley. Somehow I pressed it, letting down wheels. Somehow I pushed it across the floor. Somehow I slammed it through the double doors.

Two words flashed through the fog of my mind. *The others.* I rammed the trolley Grand Prix-style down the corridor. I stopped at the store room and slid back the bolt.

We sat in the car waiting for the back-up from Rathboyle.

'Look,' I whispered, shaking Sergeant Barry's shoulder. The light had gone on over the door of the IRC. I grabbed the torch from the back seat and trained it on the figure coming out.

He looked familiar. Of course! I'd seen him waiting outside school. 'Mr Pardoe!' He slammed the door, ran across the courtyard, took a key from his pocket and unlocked the gate.

Sergeant Barry opened the driver's door and lumbered out. 'Stop!' he shouted. But Mr Pardoe shot straight past and vanished into the woods. 'Gardaí!' the sergeant roared, clomping after him.

With the torch in my hand I ran through the open gate. Mr Geraghty followed. At the front door I punched in the code.

'How do you know —?' He broke off as the door opened.

Two women were running towards us down a corridor. One wore a cone-shaped hat. The other was handcuffed. There was a huge bruise on the right side of her face. I recognised her as the gatekeeper who'd fallen for our Trojan trick.

Behind them came a trolley, pushed by two people. The man was bare-chested. And the boy . . . well I won't go all sappy, but let's just say I've never been so glad to see anyone in my life.

DEAD MAN WALKING

'Fire!' I croaked as Charlotte and the man beside her rushed to help us with the trolley. We wheeled it across the courtyard and through the gate, stopping on the path. I couldn't tell if I was shivering from cold (I was still in my socks) or heat (my throat was burning) or fear (Mum wasn't moving).

'Ambulance,' I wheezed, pointing at the trolley.

'There's one coming,' Charlotte said. 'And a fire engine.' She trained her torch on Mum. 'What happened?'

She started to cry. Mum still lay on her side. Her eyes were closed and foam bubbled from her lips.

'Fire extinguisher. In her mouth.' I took deep gulps of freezing air to chase out the fumes.

Charlotte glanced at Mum's back and the handcuffs round her wrists. She turned to the stranger who was gawping behind her. 'Go and give that man your coat.'

He nodded, dazed, and turned to the car, where Nikos was huddling with Isla and Dana.

'Quick,' Charlotte whispered, 'we need to hide those.' She took off her hat and tucked it round Mum's wrists and hands, covering her scales and claws. I looked over to Nikos. Thank goodness he had both slippers back on which, I now noticed, were oddly rounded ankle boots.

'Who are those people?' Charlotte said.

I coughed. 'Later.' I turned to the burning building. There's someone still in there.'

She grabbed my sleeve. 'Don't you dare!'

But I didn't *not* dare. This was my fault. I'd driven a madman over the edge. He really believed it was right to sacrifice Mum: that by killing one human he'd save humankind. Well, maybe he could justify murder, but I couldn't – because murder it would be if I left him to die in a fire that I'd caused.

But there was no time to explain all that to Charlotte. So I yanked my arm free and ran back through the gate.

I said a big fat swear word, put the torch in my pocket and followed.

The fumes got stronger down the corridor, a sick solid smell that coated my throat. Passing the store room, I grabbed the fire extinguisher that Dr Krinsky had dropped after taping Mum's mouth.

We pushed through the double doors into a wall of heat. I sprayed foam at the floor, though most of the fires had burned themselves out. Either that or Dr Krinsky had quenched them before he . . . I tried not to think as I ran to the room at the back.

Charlotte followed me through the door. 'What's that?' she gasped, seeing the cage with the dead bird. 'And that?' She pointed to a notebook slotted between two bars of the cage. She pulled it out and stared at the cover.

But I was staring at something else. Against the left-hand wall was a big metal sink, like a feeding trough with taps. Beside that was a door, then a shelf of green clothes folded neatly: spare medical scrubs for Dr Krinsky.

Scrubs that he'd never wear. I pressed a fist to my mouth. On the floor beneath the shelf was a corpse. Wisps of smoke curled from its tattered black clothes. It lay on its back with the elbows bent and the fists clenched, as if the doctor had died cheering on his favourite team. He must have run in here to try and douse his clothes in the sink. I let out a sob and tried to turn Charlotte's head away.

Too late.

'Who . . .?' Tears rolled down her cheeks.

'He – he tried to kill Mum. He was starting to take out her lungs. She – I – started a fire to stop him.' The awful symmetry hit me. 'And I killed *him* instead.'

'Oh.' Charlotte looked so horrified you'd think

she was the murderer. 'Oh no.' She laid a hand on my arm. 'You had no choice, Aidan.' She bit her lip and looked back at the corpse. 'What else could you . . .'

She clamped my arm. '*LOOK!*'

My heart flipped over.

The first finger on the corpse's right hand was twitching. Now the second finger. Now the third. I would have screamed if my voice was working.

The right hand opened, then the left. Charlotte shrank behind me. The arms went straight either side. The feet wiggled. And the legs . . . the legs *bent up at the knees!*

Before we could run – as *if* we could run – he stood up. Ash flaked off him, leaving a dusty, soot-streaked . . . what? He *looked* alive. More alive than ever, in fact. Beneath the grime his face glowed as if dawn was breaking through the darkness of his cheeks.

He opened his hands and stared at the palms. 'Jeez,' he whispered. 'It worked.' His voice was dusty dry. 'It actually worked.'

He blinked round the room in bright-eyed wonder. They settled on me with the slow surprise of someone waking from sleep. 'Hey, kiddo.' He gave a black thumbs-up. 'Good job. I planned on burning down the building myself when I was done, get rid of the evidence. Thanks for helping me.' He laughed. 'Though I doubt you were trying to.'

If I'd had any words, they wouldn't come out.

He turned to the cage. 'We did it, Hessie. Can you believe we did it?' He opened the cage door, reached in a hand and lifted out the bird. Cradling it in both hands, he brought the bundle to his lips. 'Your blood saved my life,' he murmured, kissing the glittering feathers. 'Your blood *gave* me life, dear Hestia.'

'Hestia?' Charlotte whispered over my shoulder.

I glanced round at her. Were fumes cooking my brain, or had she too just seen a dead man stand up? A man who was becoming less dead by the second. Whistling, he put the bird back in the cage. Then he brushed off his sleeves, sending up clouds of ash.

A tiny voice rose out of me. 'What's happening?'

'Hestia,' Charlotte breathed again. 'The Greek goddess of fire. A fire bird.'

And suddenly I knew. Not an Amazonian parrot. Not a pet killed in rage. Somewhere, somehow, Dr Krinsky had found the mythical bird that dies in flames and rises from the ashes.

'A phoenix,' I gasped. 'You drank its blood.'

He whooped. 'Ten outta ten. Say hi to a living legend.' He gave a sweeping bow.

My terror turned to anger. 'Whoever you're working for, you've gone way too far.'

'Not far enough, kiddo.' Grinning his dazzling grin, he stepped forward. He shoved me against

Charlotte and strode to the back of the door. He came back dragging a white cloak. It was wide and curved at one end. The other end forked to two points like a tailcoat. He hauled it towards the door by the sink. As he turned the handle, the terrible truth hit.

'Wings,' I whispered. 'Nikos's wings.'

'What?' My brain was turning to cookie dough. 'Who's Nikos? *Wait!*' I took the torch from my pocket and followed Aidan through the door.

THE DREAM'S OVER

I froze in the torch light. Dr Krinsky stood ten steps in front of me on a patch of scrubby ground. In front of *him* stood – nothing. At least, nothing I could see. There was a faint, rhythmic roar from below and a salty taste in the air. My stomach lurched. He was standing on a cliff edge! The woods at the front had hidden the building's craggy location.

Dr Krinsky bent down. He fiddled with the front of the wings, untangling a set of straps.

No. He couldn't be serious.

I stepped forward. Cold ached up through my socks. I took a deep breath and spoke as calmly as I could. 'Those wings belong to Nikos, Dr Krinsky. They're part of him. They *grew* with him.' Gusts of freezing wind snatched at my words. 'You're a different height and weight. You can't just strap them on and fly.'

He looked up, shielding his eyes against the glare of Charlotte's torch.

'You think I haven't done the math? Even if I'm wrong, so what? If I die, I rise again. You've seen it for yourself. And if I so much as stub my toe, I've got my lump of alicorn to heal me.'

Despite everything, I felt cold tears on my cheeks for this desperate, deluded man. 'Don't you see, Doctor? No one's going to back you now. Your dream's over. You can't save humanity.'

His laughter danced on the wind. 'Humanity? You really bought that crap? You're the dreamer, kiddo.'

My blood turned to ice. 'What?'

'Human beings – what a lousy design. Two crummy legs that tie us to the ground. Nothing to fight with but fists and feet. And if disease doesn't get ya, death will. Two hundred thousand years on earth and that's the best we can do? Gimme a break.' He stood up. 'But every now and then, someone special turns up. A Leonardo. An Einstein.' He heaved the wings on to his back. 'A me.' The feathers framed him in a milky glow, the halo of a filthy angel. 'Someone super-smart.' He pulled a pair of wing straps forward and clipped them together in a big metal clasp round his chest. 'Someone who's born to rule. To *rewrite* the rules. Someone who's worthy of flying and living for ever.'

It felt like he'd punched a hole right through

me. 'You mean, all along you've wanted their gifts just for you?'

He clasped a second pair of straps round his left arm.

'Not wanted. Deserved.' He clipped another pair round his right arm. 'Just like I deserve to breathe fire. That'll have to wait. But I've drunk phoenix blood, got my unicorn horn and my flying gear. Three outta four ain't bad, hey kiddo?'

Something rushed through me. To call it anger would be like calling a tornado a breeze, or a tiger a cat. It was wild, unstoppable.

I stood in the doorway, transfixed by the winged madman who was turning his back on us.

There were footsteps behind. I spun round. A man in a fire suit was running towards me, gabbling into a walkie-talkie. He caught my arm.

'You OK, love?'

I snatched the walkie-talkie from his hand and yelled into the mouthpiece, 'Get the coastguard! There's a man about to fly — fall — off the cliff above the IRC.'

The fireman stared past me, his mouth open. I spun round. My body turned into a scream.

FLYING

It wasn't me who jumped on to Dr Krinsky's back. It was pure, blazing fury in the shape of a boy. I gripped my arms round his neck and buried my face in the heartbreaking softness of Nikos's wings. We perched on the edge of everything.

Then we fell.

I had no plan. I didn't even have a brain any more, just a fury-fuelled strength that drove my hands to hit and my legs to kick. But he was stronger. He wriggled his back until I lost my grip and slipped round his shoulders. Even through the icy wind, I smelt the sourness of his burnt skin. We fought and tumbled, faster and faster, me grabbing at anything – his neck, his shoulders, his arms – while he tried to shake me off. At last my fingers found the wing strap round his chest. I dangled vertically as we dived through the night. The moon and stars wobbled below us in the mirror of the sea. It glittered like coal, closer and closer and . . . SMACK! My feet hit the water. Waves

slapped my ankles, my shins, my knees and . . .
WHOOSH! Up we rose, climbing the darkness.
I heard a muffled whoop. Dr Krinsky's maths was
right. Even with me on board, he was flying. My
fingers gripped the straps in freezing agony as he
flapped his arms, letting the mighty wings work
the air currents. He swooped and soared, banked
and turned, now skimming my socks on the water,
now jolting me upwards. The wind whacked like
great sheets of invisible cardboard, jerking my
body this way and that. He was playing with me,
a mouse in his catty jaws, on his way to – where?
Did he really think he'd make it right across the
Atlantic to America? Course he did! Nothing was
impossible in his megalomaniac brain. And that
made my choice impossible: to stay here clinging
on, or let go and drown. Either way he'd win.

Which simply can't happen, said the fury that used
to be me.

I waited for a current of air to tilt Dr Krinsky
forward. Bending my knees, I slammed my feet
against his chest. My arms were stiff with cold and
the ache of hanging on. But somehow my hand
found its way up his arm to the clasp of his right
wing. And then, as if my brain had moved to my
fingers, they worked and wriggled, fumbled and
fiddled and snapped the clasp open. There was a
shriek. Together we crashed, slap-smack, into the
sea.

The cold screamed through me. The water felt solid, a monstrous black bear crushing air from my lungs. I sank, spluttering and gulping. My head came up into a strange golden light. It danced on the water, fuzzy and soft, inviting me to stop fighting, to give up and in to the waves.

A whack in the face brought me back. It was the edge of the wing I'd unstrapped. Dr Krinsky thrashed beside me, trying to undo the clasp at his chest and escape the harness. With the last of my strength I tugged. One, two . . . the loose wing jerked free. I hauled myself on to the feathery raft. Bathed in the golden halo, I heard the booming voice of an angel. And then I heard nothing.

I saw it all from the cliff top. The flight of a giant, four-legged bird, diving and soaring beneath brilliant, angry stars. The crash into the sea. The lifeboat that chugged into view. The torch beam that lit up the swimmers. Aidan freeing the wing and collapsing on top. I heard the coastguard through the loudspeaker: 'We've got you. Don't move.'

He didn't.

'No!' I howled as his body was lifted on to the boat. The prow turned towards the doctor. It looked as if he was trying to swim away. He flopped and flapped like a great wounded bird, dragging his one wing behind. And then he disappeared.

He was swallowed in one gulp. The sea closed over him, leaving nothing but the smacking lips of a million waves.

I felt an arm across my shoulder. 'Come on, love.' The fireman turned me round and steered me back through the little room, the big room, the corridor, the front door, then across the courtyard and through the gate.

Mr Geraghty ran up. 'Oh, thank goodness you're OK.' He hugged me.

OK? I burst into tears.

A fire engine and ambulance had arrived, along with a second garda car. Sergeant Barry was back from the woods and stood talking to two other guards. There was no sign of Mr Pardoe. He saw me and hurried over.

Two men were lifting Mrs Mooney on a stretcher into the ambulance.

'I have to go with her,' I sobbed.

For once Sergeant Barry didn't ask questions. 'You go too, Joe. Look after Cassandra.'

The Trojan-trick woman was holding an oxygen mask over Mrs Mooney's face. And now — oh no — she was climbing into the ambulance too.

'She can't come,' I said to Garda Barry. 'Tell her.'

The woman turned round and looked straight at me. 'I'm a nurse. I can help.' Was that a twitch of her eyelid or a wink? 'In every way.'

And she did. As we drove down the hill, one of the paramedics leaned over to remove the hat covering Mrs Mooney's hands.

'Leave it!' the nurse said in a voice like a slap. 'You'll hurt her more. The hands are badly bruised. I'll see to them later.'

But later worried me. Later meant X-rays and blood pressure monitors round scaly wrists. Later meant discovery.

The nurse didn't look the huggable type. But when we arrived at Galway Accident and Emergency, and she announced in a voice like Zeus that, 'She's stabilised but we can't risk hospital infection. I'll take her home and look after her myself.' I found my arms reaching round her. And when a doctor told me that the boy found at sea was 'on Ward 6 being treated for hypothermia', I found myself hugging him too.

DON'T MENTION IT

I told you flying was overrated. I mean, superpowers are supposed to be fun. They're not meant to give you shivers and bruises and leg pains and arm aches and headaches and a good few minutes of wondering where you are.

That's how I felt waking up in hospital next morning. Starving too, once my stomach muscles relaxed, which they only did when I heard that Mum was recovering at Dana's house.

'Dana O'Rourke was the head nurse here until a couple of weeks ago,' the doctor said. He had a kind, wrinkled face beneath a muddle of wispy hair: the opposite of Dr Krinsky, as if God had cobbled him together from the leftovers. He took my temperature and blood pressure. 'All clear, young man.' He patted my shoulder. 'You can go home. There's someone here to collect you.' He shuffled to the door.

'Can I have breakfast first?' I asked.

'Great to see you too,' Charlotte said, marching in as the doctor went out. 'And really, don't mention it. Saving your life was no bother.'

'What?' I sat bolt upright. 'I didn't know.'

Her Gorgon-face softened. 'No one told you? Oh, I suppose I'll let you off, then.' She told me how she'd called the coastguard and watched from the clifftop as the boat rescued me. 'But Dr Krinsky...' She shook her head.

I opened my mouth. All that came out was, 'Wow.'

I got Dana's number from the nurse's station. They let me call from the desk.

'Your mum's doing fine,' she said down the phone. 'Sleeping like a baby. I wouldn't disturb her now. You'll see her later.'

Then I called Gramps. 'Sorry about last night,' I said.

'What was that all about? We've been worried sick. Couldn't get through to you or your mum. Where are you?'

'Safe,' I said. 'Everything's fine. I've got to go, Gramps. I'll call you when we get home later and explain ev–' I bit my bottom lip. No way would I freak him out with the whole story. But I'd had enough of lying too: '– stuff.'

There was a man waiting with Charlotte at the entrance, the one who'd been outside the IRC last night. He was bald and smiley. 'So glad you're

OK,' he said, shaking my hand like I'd won the All Ireland Not-Drowning Championship – which, by the sound of it, I pretty much had.

'This is Aidan,' Charlotte said. 'And this is Mr Geraghty.'

'And this,' he said to me, tapping her shoulder, 'is your knightess in shining armour. Aren't you, Cassandra?'

'Cassandra?' I burst out laughing.

'Long story,' she said, glaring at me. 'But not as long as yours, I bet.'

'Later,' I mouthed.

Mr Geraghty drove us to Boonkilly and Geraghty's Store 'n' More, where Charlotte said she'd spent the night. Mrs Geraghty – 'Call me Maura' – was waiting at the door with a smile as big as her face. She squeezed my hand and led us through to the back room.

While I tucked into a mountain of porridge, she said to Charlotte, 'I knew you were pulling my leg last night.' She beamed as if her leg was proud of it. 'Now.' She folded her arms and raised her eyebrows.

'No, wait,' Mr Geraghty said. 'Liam phoned. He's on his way with that nurse. He needs to talk to them all in confidence. How about a fry-up, Maura? I'll see to the shop.'

When they'd gone, I whispered, 'Well?'

Talk about stranger than fiction. I lost count of my

squeaks as Aidan filled me in on Mr Pardoe's kidnap and Dr Krinsky's pretend-plan. When he got to Nikos, the squeak became a shriek. 'You mean actual Pegasus wings?'

He nodded.

'As in actual Pegasuses?'

I gave her my snootiest Charlotte-look. 'I think you'll find,' I said, 'it's Pegasi.'

For once in my life, I didn't mind being corrected.

RIGHT AS RAIN

Mr Geraghty came back from the shop, followed by a guard with a big red face, followed by Dana with a bruised one. I swear the fire extinguisher had invented new colours on her cheek.

'Aidan!' She rushed over and clamped me in her arms like a nut in a cracker.

'How's Mum?' I said.

'Still sleeping. I'll take you over when we're done here.'

Mr Geraghty went back to supervise the shop.

The guard came over. 'You must be Aidan,' he said. 'I'm Sergeant Barry. I hear you had a narrow escape, so.'

He put a heavy hand on my shoulder. Then he sat down opposite me and reached into his pocket.

Oh no. Interrogation time. But instead of a notepad, he pulled out a piece of paper, folded small, and passed it to me.

'From your friends – that man and lady. I invited them to stay last night but they preferred a bed and breakfast in Rathboyle. I think she was a bit shy about her, ah,' he cleared his throat, 'growth.'

'Yes,' I said. 'It's a very rare condition.' Which again wasn't a lie.

I unfolded the paper:

Dear Aidan,

Are you OK? The policeman's just had a call to say you're recovering in hospital after being rescued at sea. We can only guess what happened, and only thank you with all our hearts for saving us from the fire etc. All we ask is that you say no more than is necessary. Contact us when you can through my parents' home number in Scotland. 0044-131-6392217.

With all our thanks and love,

I & N

Sergeant Barry looked at his watch. 'They'll be here at eleven,' he said, 'to answer some questions.'

But I knew they wouldn't. I knew they'd be on their way, right now, to somewhere he'd never find. I knew that Isla had written that veiled letter in case he read it. With its 'etc' and 'no more than is necessary' it gave away nothing. And her parents' number meant that *I* could contact her but the guards, if they phoned, would be put off the scent.

'While we're waiting,' Sergeant Barry said, 'you can tell me your side of things.' And now he did pull out a notepad.

I looked desperately at Charlotte.

'Actually,' she said, 'maybe you can tell us *yours*.' The sergeant frowned.

'I found this,' she said, 'in the IRC.' She turned to her coat, draped over the back of her chair, and took something out. It was the notebook she'd found tucked through the bars of the birdcage. She held up the singed cover.

OPERATION ZOE
The Diary of a Visionary
A gift to the world in the event of my death by
DOCTOR LEVITICUS KRINSKY III
M.D, M.S, D.M.D, F.A.A.D, F.A.C.E.P

Sergeant Barry reached out to take it. But she whisked it under the table, shaking her head. 'I read it last night. And it mentions you. At least, it mentions a Sergeant Barry who was happy to take a bribe for turning a blind eye.' She tapped her forehead. 'Oh, silly me. Maybe there's another Sergeant Barry who's in charge of the nearest garda station. I didn't think of that.' She blinked at him with her great big eyes.

His red face went even redder. 'I didn't take a cent.'

'No, but you agreed to, which is just as bad. And I've got the proof here.'

'What do you want?' he muttered.

'The same thing as you,' Charlotte said. 'That we all keep quiet about this. That you tell everyone that there was a fire at the government research place; that everything was destroyed; that somebody fell off the cliff and drowned; and that nothing more is known.'

His face seemed to crumple. 'Mrs B and I haven't had a holiday in years. I was planning a Bermuda surprise. I didn't think a gift would do any harm, especially when I believed him. I thought his CIA papers were on their way.'

Dana sat down next to him. 'Don't feel too bad. I was duped too. I saw an ad in the paper: "Exciting opportunity for an experienced nurse."' She shook her head. 'He brainwashed me with his lie about saving humanity.'

'You and everyone else,' I said. 'Mum, Nikos, Isla, even me for a bit.' I left out Mr Pardoe. Partly because I didn't know how washed his brain actually was – he'd stood by while Nikos had been tortured and Mum nearly murdered, after all – but mostly because I didn't want the gardaí to go looking for him. If he was arrested, he might start blabbing things he shouldn't.

The Geraghtys came in with plates of bacon, egg, sausages, fried bread, mushrooms and black and white pudding.

But I wasn't hungry. I turned to Dana. 'Can we go now? I want to see Mum. Will she be OK?'

Dana nodded. 'Plenty of rest and she'll be right as rain.'

She meant it well, she really did. But when you think about it, there's a lot that isn't right about rain.

SILENCE

A week later, I was in the kitchen making honey-raisin-avocado ice-cream. I knew honey and ice-cream were good for throats; people eat them after they've had their tonsils out. And avocado is smooth and nutritious, just the thing to heal damaged airways like Mum's.

Forget that. No-one has airways like Mum's. Anyway, I was spooning some into a bowl when the doorbell rang.

'In time for a treat,' I said, closing the door behind Charlotte.

She followed me to the kitchen and looked at the ice-cream. 'How is she? Can I take that up to her?'

I nodded.

She stopped at the foot of the stairs. 'Has she said anything?'

I shook my head. 'How's school?'

'Boring.' Charlotte grinned. 'Which is just fine after last weekend.' She'd gone back on Thursday after three days of 'flu'. Mine had lasted the whole week since our return last Sunday afternoon.

We slept the whole way back from Boonkilly, Mrs Mooney in the front seat, me and Aidan in the back. Dana dropped me home first. When Dad got in from his shift at twenty past seven, I'd showered and washed my muddy clothes in the machine to avoid any awkward questions.

'Had fun at Aidan's?' He kissed my forehead. 'I missed you.'

'Me too.' I buried my head in the dadness of his jumper so he wouldn't hear the catch in my voice. And that, as far as he knew, was that.

We went upstairs to Mum's room. She was sitting in bed reading. She patted the duvet. We perched on the edge of the bed. Her breath came in little rasps, like a kettle just after it's boiled. She ate a spoonful of ice-cream.

'Marks out of ten?' I said. She held up ten claws.

'Guess the flavour.'

She took another bite, frowning. When I told her, she smiled and clicked her tongue, as if she should have known.

'Are you feeling better?' Charlotte said. Mum did a thumb-claws up.

'Do you want anything else?' I said.

She thought for a minute. Then she shook her head, lay back on the pillow and closed her eyes. Shaking my head at Charlotte, I eased the bowl from her claws. We went out, closing the door softly.

Since waking up a week ago, Mum hadn't said a word.

I went back to school on Monday. Nothing had changed. Why would it? I'd only been away for a week. There was the map of Ireland on the wall with the rip through West Cork. There was the list of class rules above Miss Burkitt's desk: 'Listen to others. Use kind words. Try your best.'

And everything had changed. It's hard to describe, but I felt deeper and calmer and more complicated, as if the ocean was still inside me, swilling about.

At least, that's how I felt until break. I was heading into the yard when I felt a tap on my arm.

'Aidan?'

I turned round. Phil looked smaller than ten days ago. His shoulders were hunched, his face all pinched.

'What's going on? My dad hasn't come home since I told you all that stuff. He phoned Mum to say his work trip was extended. Then you were away too, so I know it's got something to do with your family.'

'You're dead right. After your dad kidnapped my mum, that American man who visited your house tried to kill her so that he could breathe fire, and he also took some horn from a unicorn lady and cut the wings off a Pegasus man and then he died in a fire, but he rose again because he'd drunk phoenix blood, and he flew away, so I jumped on his back and fell into the Atlantic Ocean and nearly drowned.'

I didn't say that. But I did give him a message for his dad. With my fist.

When I came home that afternoon, Mum was waiting at the door. I hugged her so tightly she wheezed like a mouth organ.

'Sorry.' I stepped back. 'You're better, Mum!' She nodded and smiled. My heart sank. When would she talk again?

I guess that depends what you mean by talking. Because what, actually, is a voice? Is it the sound that leaves your mouth as speech or song? Is it the tone of that sound: loud or soft, a Miss Burkitt bark or a Charlotte squeak? Is it the equipment – your voice box or tongue or teeth – that shapes the sound into 'Hello' or 'Ouch!' or 'I'll have the Caramel Chew Chew'? Is it the air dancing from your lungs and out?

It's all that and more. It has to be because Mum no longer speaks or sings, not loudly or softly or squeakily. The air doesn't dance but whistles from her mouth and nostrils.

But she talks in other ways – with her hands and her hugs and her gossipy eyes. And now that I have to work harder to understand her, I'm noticing other things too. Perhaps before I was so hung up on her dragony bits that I never really saw her perfect oval yawn, or the way she drinks tea with the bag still in, or how her ears go up when she smiles. Those things and more make her my amazing, one-off mum, just as much as the way she breathed fire.

Yes, *breathed*. We think it might be over. Something inside her must have been destroyed by the fire extinguisher foam because there hasn't been the teeniest spark in the month since our adventure. That's what we're calling it, by the way. Not a disaster or a tragedy because there were some good bits too.

Like Nikos and Isla getting engaged only two weeks after they met. How violinny is that? And the way he can walk around now without people staring at his 'hunchback'. Isla's even had the courage to go out and about with him a few times. In her hat, of course. She's thinking of giving a sample of alicorn for medical research. Not for a while, though, and anonymously, and only if she can find a good scientist who'll use it properly, not another wicked, power-hungry ego-on-legs like Dr Krinsky.

DROWN AND OUT

Charlotte's right about the ego-on-legs. It could have walked Dr Krinsky to Australia, judging by his diary. He must have shoved it between the bars of Hestia's cage just before he died in the fire, so that someone would find it if the phoenix blood failed to bring him back to life. The whole thing was a massive con. He was trying to make out his aims were noble, so that he'd be remembered as a hero.

And he might have succeeded, if you hadn't survived and he hadn't been so vain. But he couldn't help showing off with his clever-clever double meanings.

Like?

The name of his project for starters. 'Operation' was more than just a James Bondy kind of word for his grand plan, as poor Nikos found out. And 'Zoe' is the Greek word for life. I bet he wanted his diary readers to think that meant all the lives on earth he was going to save. If he hadn't come clean on the clifftop, we still wouldn't know that it was only *his* life he cared about.

I'm still not sure why he did come clean.

I told you: vanity. He had his wings, his alicorn and his renewable life. He thought he'd won. All that stuff about God not existing . . . he thought *he* was God. And like any massive bighead, he just had to brag to someone about how brilliant he was. But he picked the wrong someone. He hadn't bargained on your bravery. Or stupidity. I can't quite decide.

Be careful – that was almost a compliment. Well *I* can't decide how much Mr Pardoe knew.

My guess is not the whole story. If he'd known Dr Krinsky's real motive — to grab everything — I bet he wouldn't have helped. I hope not, anyway. He'll never tell us now.

Not that he didn't try. Two days after I went back to school, Sergeant Barry phoned to say that a Mr Pardoe had walked into Rathboyle Garda Station with some crazy story about Dr Krinsky doing tests on humans with mythological features.

'Really?' I said down the phone. 'Sounds ridiculous. Let me just check in that diary Charlotte found. Maybe he mentions something after that bit he wrote about bribing you.'

There was a long silence. Then Sergeant Barry said, 'Yes, I thought this Pardoe fella seemed a bit unbalanced. We're charging him with arson. Found his fingerprints in the building. Where, by the way, we didn't find a strange dead bird in a cage. He'll be out of trouble for a good long time.'

Not as long as Dr Krinsky, though. Weighed down by the clasps of his wings, it doesn't matter how much phoenix blood he drank because there's fat chance of a fire on the seabed, which means fat chance of any ashes to rise from. And that kind of puts a damper –

Ha not-bad ha.

– on his dreams of living forever.

CHRISTMAS BAKE

It's the last day of term and Mum's had a great idea. When I got home from school yesterday, she held up a piece of paper.

How about a Christmas Baking Party?

Charlotte and I gave out invitations this morning. It was amazing. Kennedy asked if we could invent new recipes, and Andy Dunne wants to make Ancient Greek Christmas monsters.

When I told him that the Ancient Greeks didn't do Christmas, he looked disappointed. So I said why not make some for their winter festival instead, which celebrated the birth of Dionysus, god of wine and feasting.

Conor Murphy said it was the first invitation he'd had all term. That made me feel good, and a bit not-good too. I'd been so busy feeling left out of Phil's group, I hadn't even noticed that others felt the same. Now Phil was the one left out. You should have seen his face when I invited Ben and Dan and Tom.

I did. I felt sorry for him.

What?! After all he did?

It's hard not to pity someone whose dad's in prison. And when you think about it, what exactly *did* he do, except act like a moron because he wanted to be admired? And I was thinking, if this baking party works out, maybe our mum — I mean your mum — could start a cookery afterschool and everyone could come round and invent pizzas and pies and monster cakes and Easter cakes and cheesecakes and traybakes and Arctic rolls and Antarctic rolls and profiteroles and jam roly-polys and ham roly-polys…and maybe 'everyone' might include Phil Pardoe.

And maybe pigs might fly, Charlotte smarty-pants
        annoying
           squeaky
              best-friend-ever
              Flynn.

Why not? I've heard of stranger things.

BIODIVERSITY BAKING

Here are some of the recipes in the story. I don't mean to boast –

Well don't then 😞

– but they're pretty good. If you don't BELIEVE me, then why not make them yourself and mark them out of ten?

CHOCOCHILLI MAYO CAKE (page 47)

Phil Pardoe's sweet chilli sauce gives this cake the kick he deserves.

INGREDIENTS

2 cups self-raising flour

1 cup hot chocolate powder

½ cup mayonnaise

3 dessertspoons honey

1 teaspoon sweet chilli sauce

1 cup lukewarm water

DIRECTIONS

1. Preheat the oven to 180°C (gas mark 4). Line an 18 cm diameter cake tin with greaseproof paper and grease this lightly with butter.

2. Mix all the ingredients in a bowl. Spoon into the cake tin.

3. Bake in the preheated oven for about half an hour, until a dragon claw (if you don't have one, a fork will do) stuck into the centre of the cake comes out clean. Leave in the cake tin for 10 minutes before removing to cool completely on a wire rack.

CHOCOLATE CUPCAKE VAMPIRE BATS (page 75)

You can look up a chocolate cupcake recipe but I'm cheating here by using a box of chocolate cupcake mix. It's easier and quicker and leaves more time to dangle the bats from the ceiling before your family walks in for dinner. Fiddly but rewarding.

INGREDIENTS

Box of chocolate cupcake mix
Dark Halloweeny cupcake cases

Strong black cotton thread

Needle

Sellotape or Blu Tack to stick on the ceiling

Packet of plain chocolate digestives, each biscuit cut in half to make 2 semicircle wings

White jelly beans for the bats' eyes

Red jelly beans for fangs

Icing sugar to stick the wings into the sides of the cupcakes and to attach the eyes and fangs

DIRECTIONS

Make the bats' bodies

1. Preheat the oven to the temperature required on the cupcake mix box, usually about 180°C (gas mark 4). Put cupcake cases on a baking tray (the box will tell you how many).
2. Make the chocolate cupcake mix following the instructions on the box and spoon into the cases.
3. Bake for the time it gives on the box.
4. Leave the cupcakes on a wire rack to cool.

Make the eyes and (optional) fangs

a. Make icing 'glue' by adding drops of water (a tiny bit each time) to the icing sugar and stirring very well until the icing is firm and sticky. Too much water makes the icing too runny.

b. Cut a white jelly bean in half. Make 2 holes in the cupcake for eyes. Use the icing to stick in the 2 jelly bean halves for spooky white peepers.

c. For the fangs, if you've got the patience, cut little triangles out of red jelly beans (little scissors are good). Blob on icing sugar to stick them below the eyes, pointing down.

Make the wings

1. Make a slit either side of each cupcake case with a sharp knife. Use the knife to push icing in the slit.

2. Stick in the chocolate biscuit semicircles each side for wings. Leave for an hour or so until the icing hardens, to be sure the wings are stuck firmly.

The dangly bit

1. Thread a big darning needle with strong black cotton (different lengths so that the bats will hang at different heights).

2. Make a big, strong knot at one end of the cotton.

3. Cut out a circle of black card (about 2 cm diameter) and thread the cotton through. Stick the knot end of the cotton firmly to the card with Sellotape (this is a kind of plug to make sure the cotton holds the bat when it's hanging).

4. Thread the cotton through the cupcakes so that the bats' faces hang vertically and upside down.

5. Stick the top end of the cotton to the ceiling with Sellotape or Blu Tack.

COUNTRY CAKE (page 57)

Mum and I made Australia but you can adapt to your chosen country, e.g.:

France: the Eiffel Tower made from a Curly Wurly shaped at the edges into a tall triangle.

Switzerland, South America or Nepal: a length of Toblerone White for the Alps, Andes or Himalayas.

Ireland: green icing (icing sugar, water and 3 teaspoons of green food colouring). Scatter with sheep (pieces of popcorn).

Make a sugar-free sponge cake, like I do to protect Mum's teeth (remember she can't go to the dentist). Then it's so healthy you can eat a shark fin no problem.

INGREDIENTS
For Australia (sugar-free sponge cake)

150g (5oz) margarine

3 tablespoons honey

3 eggs, beaten

150g (5oz) self-raising flour

A few drops of vanilla essence

For Ayers Rock

1 big Shredded Wheat (not the little Shreddies)

Red food colouring

Cinnamon powder

For the surrounding oceans

1 big piece of blue card or blue tray

Upright triangles from a bar of Toblerone White for shark fins

DIRECTIONS
Make Australia

1. Preheat the oven to 180°C (gas mark 4).
2. Melt the margarine and honey in a pan over a gentle heat.

3. Sieve the flour into a large bowl. Stir in the pan contents.

4. Add the beaten eggs and mix.

5. Spoon the mixture into a round (18 cm diameter) cake tin.

6. Bake for about half an hour until a fork or dragon claw stuck into the cake comes out clean.

7. Cool the cake for 5 minutes or so, then turn on to a rack.

8. When the cake is completely cool, find a map of Australia. With Mum's claw (or a sharp knife) carve the cake edge into the shape of the coastline. Place on a big piece of blue card or a blue tray. Cut out individual triangles from the Toblerone White and stand them upright on the blue card/tray for shark fins.

Make Ayers Rock

1. Take 1 Shredded Wheat and dip it in a bowl of red food colouring. Leave it to dry for about 5 minutes.

2. Sprinkle with cinnamon.

3. Put roughly in the middle of the Australia cake (look on the map to place it properly).

CRUNCHIE BAR-NANA BREAD (page 64)

**A great way to eat chocolate – mixed with
healthy fruit so your parents can't complain.**

INGREDIENTS

3 ripe bananas, peeled

⅓ cup melted butter

1 teaspoon baking powder

Pinch of salt

1 large egg, beaten

1 Crunchie bar

1½ cups plain flour

DIRECTIONS

Method

1. Preheat the oven to 180°C (gas mark 4). Grease a 10 x 20 cm loaf tin with butter.
2. In a mixing bowl, mash the bananas with a fork until smooth (add a spoonful of boiling water from the kettle if necessary). Pour in the melted butter.
3. Mix in the baking powder and salt.
4. Add the beaten egg.
5. Break the Crunchie Bar into little chunks and stir into the mixture.

6. Add the flour and mix well.
7. Pour the batter into your prepared loaf tin. Bake for 50 minutes to 1 hour or until a fork or claw in the centre comes out clean.
8. Remove from the oven and cool in the tin.
9. Take the bread out, slice up and eat (probably the whole loaf in one go).

FIRST DAY FLAPJACKS (page 20)

Perfect for celebrating first-time events: first day of term, first day of the holidays, first time you watch *Star Wars*, though NOT first day of wearing braces. And by the way, I tweaked the recipe since my first day at school so they're crunchy and happy, not soggy and sad.

INGREDIENTS

110g butter
2 tablespoons golden syrup
175g porridge oats
50g sultanas or raisins (optional)
30ml neat Ribena

DIRECTIONS

1. Preheat the oven to 180°C (gas mark 4). Line a rectangular baking tray (about 35 x 25 cm)

with greaseproof paper and grease with a little butter.

2. Put the butter and golden syrup in a saucepan. Put on a low heat and mix till it has melted and the sugar has dissolved.

3. Take it off the heat and add the oats and the fruit if wanted. Mix well till the oats are coated (if not, add a little more golden syrup).

4. Add the Ribena and mix well.

5. Pour the mixture into the greased tin. Flatten down with the back of a spoon.

6. Place the flapjack in the oven for 10 to 20 minutes until golden brown on the top.

7. Leave to cool for 5 minutes then divide into slices with a knife. Leave to cool completely, separating the slices.

GORGON CAKE (page 100)

Turn annoying teachers and Pardoes to stone with this sneaky, snaky bake.

INGREDIENTS

For the gorgon head

See ingredients for the Country cake (page 246)

For the hair

Strawberry laces

Icing sugar

For the face

Glacier mints

Red boiled sweet (optional)

DIRECTIONS

For the gorgon head

Make the same round sugar-free sponge cake described above for the Country cake (page 246).

For the hair

When the cake has cooled completely, stick strawberry laces around the top with icing sugar (you can add some sour worms for an extra-snaky look).

For the face

Make two eye holes in the cake and press a glacier mint into each.

For the mouth, you could use a round, red boiled sweet for an O-shaped look of doom, or strawberry laces arranged in the shape of thin, mean lips.

HONEY-RAISIN-AVOCADO ICE-CREAM (page 232)

Perfect for hot days, parties and the throats of part-dragons damaged by fire extinguisher foam.

INGREDIENTS

2 large, ripe avocados
1 can (395g) condensed milk
1½ cups double cream
2 tablespoons honey
Handful of raisins
Sealable freezer bag

DIRECTIONS

1. Peel the avocados and put the flesh in a food processor.
2. Add the condensed milk, double cream, honey and raisins. Mix until smooth.
3. Spoon the mixture into a freezer bag, squeeze out any extra air and seal the bag. Lay flat in the freezer for 2 to 3 hours until almost firm.
4. Remove from the bag and break into chunks. Return the green mixture to the food processor and blend until smooth.
5. Spoon the mixture into a loaf tin or an airtight container with a tight-fitting lid (an old ice cream box will do). Cover the mixture with plastic wrap, pressing it down on the surface. Then put on the container lid, making sure it's sealed properly.
6. Freeze for another 4 to 5 hours or until the ice cream is firm.

HULA HOOP CUPCAKES _(page 64)

It's all about expectation. Forget that cupcakes are meant to be sweet and you'll love these cheesy crunchers.

INGREDIENTS

250g self-raising flour
2 teaspoons baking powder
50g butter
1 egg
250ml milk
100g grated Cheddar cheese
A small bag of plain Hula Hoops
Pinch of salt

DIRECTIONS

1. Preheat the oven to 220°C (gas mark 7). Put 12 cupcake cases on a tray.
2. Sift the flour, baking powder and salt into a big bowl.
3. Rub in the butter with your finger/claw tips.
4. Crush the Hula Hoops on a tray with a rolling pin into coarse crumbs.
5. Add them to the bowl and mix well.
6. Add the egg, milk and cheese.
7. Spoon the mixture into the cupcake cases.
8. Bake for 25 minutes.

MUTANT SPIDER CAKE (page 75)

Great for Halloween and the chairs of annoying teachers.

INGREDIENTS

For the spider's cakey body
See ingredients for the Chocochilli mayo cake (page 242)

For the eyes
Bag of white jelly beans

For the legs
9 or more chocolate Matchmakers (or you can un-ravel liquorice spirals to make bendy legs, which somehow look more mutant)

For the blood sauce
Custard powder
Milk
Red food colouring
Cocoa powder (optional)

DIRECTIONS

For the spider

1. Make the round Chocochilli mayo cake (page

242). Add an extra teaspoon of sweet chilli sauce to give a Halloween fright to the taste buds.

2. Carve the circular cake into a weird mutant shape for the spider's body.
3. Stick on 8 white jelly beans for the spider's eyes (or more, to make it really mutant) with icing.
4. Stick 9 or more chocolate Matchmakers into the sides of the cake (again, more legs, more mutant).

For the blood sauce

1. Make the custard (follow directions on the packet).
2. Add 2 tablespoons red food colouring and stir in well.
3. To make the blood extra dark and wicked, add a tablespoon of cocoa powder.

MYSTERY MUFFINS (page 96)

Give these to someone who hates vegetables without telling them the mystery ingredient. Get them to give a mark out of ten, then tell them and see if they run for the bathroom.

INGREDIENTS

150g self-raising flour

75g porridge oats

2 teaspoons cinnamon

50g granulated sugar

1 teaspoon baking powder

½ teaspoon bicarbonate soda

1 kiwi fruit, peeled and chopped small

Mystery ingredient: 100g courgettes grated (leave the skin on)

75ml milk

1 egg

2 tablespoons water

DIRECTIONS

1. Preheat the oven to 180°C (gas mark 4). Put 12 muffin cases in a tin.
2. Mix the dry ingredients in a bowl.
3. Peel the kiwi fruit, chop into small pieces and add.
4. Grate the courgette and add.
5. Mix the milk, egg and water together then stir into the mixture.
6. Spoon the mixture into the muffin cases. Put in the oven and bake for half an hour.
7. Serve.

PEAWURLY COOKIES _(page 59)

Charlotte said these look like baked dog poop. Mention this before offering them round and there'll be more for you.

INGREDIENTS

1 cup butter

1 cup smooth peanut butter

2 eggs

2 cups self-raising flour

1 teaspoon baking powder

Pinch of salt

2 Curly Wurlys, chopped into small pieces

DIRECTIONS

1. Mix the butter and peanut butter together in a bowl.
2. Beat in the eggs.
3. Add the chopped Curly Wurly pieces and mix in well with a metal spoon.
4. In a separate bowl, sift the flour, baking powder and salt.
5. Add this to the butter mixture. Press into a dough. Add a few drops of water if necessary to make the dough stick together.
6. Put the dough in the fridge and leave for an hour.

7. Preheat the oven to 180°C (gas mark 4). Line a baking tin with greaseproof paper and grease this lightly with butter.
8. Roll the cookie dough into 1 inch balls and put on the baking tray, well spread apart.
9. Flatten each side with the side of a knife.
10. Bake for about 10 minutes or until cookies look like you-know-what.

PHIL PARDOE PIE (page 52)

You can change the pie filling to match the first letter of your own name (I use apples, apricots, Aero bar and almonds. Lucky Charlotte – chocolate, Cheerios, cherries, cream and custard).

INGREDIENTS

For the pastry
1 cup plain flour
½ cup porridge oats
75g butter chopped into small cubes
50g peanut butter
1 handful butter popcorn
1 egg yolk
2–3 tablespoons water

For the pie filling
1–2 cans (450g) of tinned peaches, depending on how peachy you want it

DIRECTIONS

Make the pastry

1. Grease a pie dish (roughly 20 cm diameter) with butter.

2. Combine the flour, porridge oats, butter, peanut butter and popcorn in a food processor. Mix until it looks like breadcrumbs. Add the egg yolk and water. Knead until the dough comes together.

3. Squash it into a ball, wrap in cling film and leave in the fridge for half an hour.

4. Preheat the oven to 180°C (gas mark 4).

5. Sprinkle a little flour on a clean surface and roll out just over half the pastry to about 3 mm thick.

6. Fit this into the bottom of the pie dish and up the sides. Trim the edges round the rim of the dish.

Make the filling and pie

1. Drain most of the syrup from the tin of peaches

2. Add peaches to the pastry base of the pie in the dish.

3. Roll out the rest of the pastry on a lightly floured surface to make the pie lid.

4. Fit on top of the peaches, wetting the edges of the pastry where the lid fits the base to make it stick.
5. Trim with a knife.
6. Cook for half an hour or until the pastry is golden toasty brown.

ACKNOWLEDGEMENTS

A huge thank you from me, Aidan, Mum, Charlotte, and even Phil Pardoe, to:

Siobhán Parkinson, Gráinne Clear, Matthew Parkinson-Bennett and the Little Island team for your kindness, encouragement, expertise and warmth. It's a joy to visit your shores.

The Arts Council for supporting the birth of this book.

Rebecca Jones at Cornerstone for your astute guidance and for getting rid of Dad.

Jane O'Hanlon and Moira Cardiff for your energy and enthusiasm.

The pupils of Primrose Hill National School for your title advice, and Liz Butler for your great support and friendship. Charlotte Stevens, my young super-reader, as smart as your fictional namesake.

The wonderful Clondalkin crew – children, Jenny and Graham – who welcome me into your world every Monday for writing fun and games.

The children and teachers at Our Lady's Hospital School, Crumlin, who do the same on Fridays.

Mags Walsh for your generosity, encouragement and general loveliness.

Vera McEvoy for your creative, compassionate friendship, and Adam Keogh, whose kindness, patience and advice helped me into Aidan's head.

The wise and wonderful Joan Proudfoot, lovely Lisa Willson, and all the other friends in Ireland, the UK and South Africa who have encouraged me up, down and along.

Cynthia, Jenny, Hilary and families: stars across the water.

Mum, Dad and Jo for your simply tremendous love, and Iain for your kindness and fun.

Ruby, Emily and Rosa – in any order – for your beauty and hilarity on legs.

Stevie for everything.

ABOUT THE AUTHOR

Debbie Thomas has worked as a journalist in Bangladesh, where she was caught in a cyclone, and South Africa, where she swam in a crocodile-sprinkled river. Celbridge in County Kildare is the slightly safer home she now shares with her husband, three daughters and attention-seeking garden. She has written four children's books (*Dead Hairy*, *Jungle Tangle*, *Monkie Business* and *Class Act*) and is the Writer in Residence at Crumlin Hospital School. In the next three years she will write a musical, bungee jump from a bridge in Ecuador and help to start a project supporting disadvantaged children in South Africa. Honest.

ABOUT THE PUBLISHER

Based in Dublin, Little Island Books has been publishing books for children and teenagers since 2010. It is Ireland's only English-language publisher that publishes exclusively for young people. Little Island specialises in publishing new Irish writers and illustrators, and also has a commitment to publishing books in translation.

www.littleisland.ie

Little
Island